For Sandra.

Tu sei la mia vita.

Everett Cannon

ALL WAS A LIE

Bibliografische Information der Deutschen Nationalbibliothek: Die Deutsche Nationalbibliothek verzeichnet diese Publikation in der Deutschen Nationalbibliografie; detaillierte bibliografische Daten sind im Internet über http://dnb.dnb.de abrufbar.

© 2022 Everett Cannon

Cover-Design: Germancreative

Korrektorat: Precious Mutero

Herstellung und Verlag: BoD – Books on Demand, Norderstedt

ISBN: 978-3-7557-6122-8

Content

THE MASKED MAN

"Do you have any leads regarding who did this?" asks my sobbing mother.

"We are doing everything we can to find him. He couldn't have gotten far. We have the entire place surrounded. He is bound to show up soon. Your daughter is very strong to have survived as long as she did with those injuries," an officer responds.

What a load of crap. I'm not strong at all! Naive and stupid is a better description. I just hope they find him before I wake up... that's if I wake up. Is this what it feels like to be in a coma? It's the strangest thing; my mind is as active as ever, but my body is just lying here unresponsive. I can't help but think what would have happened if I had not sent that stupid text. Imagine! I am here because I sent a freaking text message. I mean how ridiculous does that sound? Let's go back to the beginning, shall we?

"Amber, are you going to the party this Friday?"

"You know I can't, Emily. My mother doesn't even let me go to school by myself, let alone a party."

"Oh, come on, Amber. You could always sneak out. I mean, we're teenagers; it's basically a rite of passage for us. Besides, how often do we get invited to a senior's party?"

"You're right!"

"It's even a masked party for crying out loud. It just screams mystery and adventure and who knows, we might even get lucky."

"Emily!"

"Oh, calm down virgin."

×××

I'm finally doing it; I'm actually sneaking out. Mother would throw a fit if she could see me now. Emily and I agreed to meet at the park so we could take a taxi together to the party. It's so cold. Why did I let her talk me into wearing this tiny dress?

Is it the fact that I don't go anywhere at night or has the park always been this creepy? I take a seat on a bench and wait for the girl who doesn't know the meaning of punctuality to arrive.

Suddenly, it feels like I have daggers on my back. I feel piercing eyes watching me from behind and this chill in the air is not helping. When you feel like you're being watched, it is usually when something bad happens. *I guess I watch way too many horror movies for my own good.*

"Boo!"

"Jesus! Emily don't do that. I thought you were gonna abduct me."

"Wow!" she laughs mockingly.

"I'm way too sexy to be a kidnapper and you watch way too many horror movies. You look so hot in that dress, though."

"You gave me the tiniest dress ever!"

"C'mon, stop complaining. Come on, let's get a taxi."

×××

We arrive at the party and I can't even recognize one person. A guy who looks way too old to be our age walks up to us and whispers something in Emily's ear. He then takes her by the hand and they leave.

"Have fun, Amber. I'll come to find you later," she yells over the deafening music.

It's strange, I don't feel so alone. If anything, I feel free. Under this mask, I can be anything. A scream jolts me from my thought. It seems to be coming from outside. *Why are there so many people gathering around... Oh no!* I get a glimpse of a bloody mask, her bloody mask. There she was sprawled on the floor unmoving.

"Emily? Emily? This can't be happening. Call 911! Why are you all just standing there? Do something!"

"Calm down; it's a prank, she's not dead. Emily, go on, tell your friend to chill. Tell her that it's just a prank," says some random person.

I start to shake her body but she just lies there unresponsive. I lean in.

"She's...not breathing... she has no pulse."

I hear screaming and shouting as people start to scatter. This isn't real, she can't be dead, can she?

×××

"Miss, Miss I'm going to have to ask you to step away from the body."

"What?"

I didn't even hear the sirens or notice the police when they came. How? This was supposed to be an epic night out for us but now it's... she's...

The police start questioning the people that were left but it seems like no one saw what happened. Suddenly, a hand squeezes something in mine.

"Don't turn around. If you want to know what happened to your friend, text this number."

×××

It's been about a week since Emily died. The police have no leads yet. My mother grounded me for the rest of my life because of what happened. She has always been paranoid, but this just set her into overdrive. I need answers but I can't find the strength to text that number. What if it is a trap? For all I know, I could be next but it's Emily. I have to know. I text:

(Me): Hello, you said to text you.

(Unknown number): It took you long enough. Meet me at the lake behind the crime scene.

(Me): You mean the house where the party was held? I didn't know there was a lake there.

×××

The lake is so beautiful. I can't believe I didn't realize it was here. In an instant, while I am viewing the beautiful lake, things change to pitch black. A bag is placed over my head, blocking my vision. There is thrashing and struggling until a sharp pain at my side jolts my action. It feels like I am being tossed into the back of a car.

"Let me out! Please let me out!"

"Silence!"

Fear is all I can feel. I don't want to die. I can't believe this is happening. The car suddenly stops and I feel rough arms drag me from inside the car. This strange person walks for what feels like thirty minutes until he stops and places me on a chair and ties my hands to it. The bag is violently pulled from my face.

"I have been watching you," the man says.

"Please, I don't know what you want from me. I promise if you release me, I wouldn't tell a soul what happened. I mean, I can't even see your face because of that mask so I can't tell who you are. Just release me please."

"Your friend didn't talk this much when I had her. She was rather cooperative when I tied her up."

"A-are you going to rape me?

"Don't think of me as some low life. Who does that?"

"Oh, just a low life who takes people against their will and kills them!" I yell angrily.

"While I do admire your feisty nature, be careful what you say to me, less you wake up John. Trust me, you wouldn't like him. Oh, and I didn't kill your friend, John did. I told him not to, but he just couldn't help it... apologies."

"W-what do you want from me?"

"I said I would tell you how your friend died, and now that I have, I want you to do something for me."

He goes into a room and comes back with a small cage-like thing.

"If it's not too much trouble, would you mind getting in?"

I look at him in disbelief like what the actual hell?

"Please don't resist. If you do, John will get angry and bad things always happen when he does."

He unties me and I notice that the door to the other room is left slightly open. I don't have time to second guess it. I turn on my heel and make my way for the door.

I wasn't prepared for what my eyes see next, T...there is blood everywhere. Body parts sprawled everywhere like a sadistic science experiment gone wrong.

"He told you not to resist, didn't he?!" The masked man shouts.

He enters the room but sounds completely different from how he was earlier. He grabs me by my neck and puts pressure on my neck. I can feel my throat close. He grabs a knife and makes a line on my forehead. I can't breathe. The blood dripping from my forehead starts to cloud my vision. I close my eyes and welcome the dark-ness.

I wake up in an enclosed space. He put me in a cage! My whole body feels like it has been pressed together for so long. I touch my forehead only to feel stitches. *Why did he cut me only to stitch me back? I wonder.*

"I'm glad to see you awake. I must apologize for what John did to you. Although, I did warn you not to make him angry."

"Why in the world are you referring to yourself in the third person? You fucking cut my forehead!"

"Darling, don't get it twisted. John did that, not me. You see, John is me but I am definitely not him."

"I don't understand how I am the one twisting things. What type of fucking psychopath are you?!"

"Psychopath? Heavens no. Would a psychopath have prepared a meal and a bath for you?"

He comes toward the cage he put me in and unlocks it. I try to stand but my legs give way and I fall on the cold ground. *How long was I cramped up in that cage?*

"Silly girl, you have been out for two days now., John was getting bored and wanted to kill you, but I stopped him. I want to have you all to myself."

"I think you understand that if you try to run, John will show you no mercy. Take a bath and eat like the good girl that I know you are."

John or not John sits down behind me, his eyes looking at me so intently. This is degrading. I can't run or do anything. I take off my clothes in front of him and enter the bathtub.

"Doesn't the water feel nice?" he asks.

I get out of the tub and he immediately comes to my side. He starts sniffing me before he dresses me with a robe.

"You smell pure... I like that."

He sets me on a chair and sits opposite me. I notice a small vase on the table near him. I need to think of a way to escape. I gently walk towards him with a smile on my face.

"I just thought we should be closer," I say, gently touching his mask.

I take the vase from the table and smash it against his head. He seems to be out cold. I start searching his body for a mobile phone. I hurriedly dial 911.

"Hi, my name is Amber. I need you to track this phone. I have just been kidnap-"

My ears start ringing. *How is he awake already?* I touch my ears and only feel a shard of glass stuck to it.

"You bitch! I knew he was too soft on you. I should have killed you when I had the chance. It doesn't matter. It will be fun watching you die from blood loss."

He picks up the phone and starts cursing before he leaves. I can barely see anything. My vision is failing me once again.

×××

"We found her; she is over here!" Yells one of the policemen.

"Stay with me, miss. Don't close your eyes."

That is the last voice I hear before my eyes betray me and close shut. *I wonder how long it has been since that day. How long I have been in a coma. Mother comes every day to see me. I wish she could hear how sorry I am. If I had just stayed at home, none of this would have happened. I could have probably talked Emily out of going to that party. We could be in her room right now laughing our asses off. Instead, she is dead and I'm here.*

"Amber, please open your eyes," mom whispers.

I try and bright light fills my vision.

"Amber? My goodness Amber."

I try to speak but my throat feels dry.

"Don't try to talk dear. Hold on; let me get the doctor."

The doctor comes in and tells my mom to please wait outside. I know I have heard this voice before. My head hurts as I try to remember where exactly I did. The doctor walks up to me with a smile on his face but something doesn't feel right.

"Hello, Amber," he speaks softly.

John?

ALICE

"Alice! Alice!" Detective James calls out to the woman seated in front of him. Her expression is significantly less frightening than it was earlier when he saw her. He had seen a lot of things in his ten years as a detective, but the sight of Alice an hour ago was alarming.

"Hmmm?" Alice snaps out of her thoughts. "I'm sorry," she says as she places her palm on her cheek.

"I was told you would not talk to anyone and specifically asked to see me?" Detective James places a notepad and a recording device on the table as he speaks. He notices Alice's attention is focused on the device. " It's a recording device. It's just to make sure I do not forget what you tell me."

Alice says nothing in response. She continues to rub her cheeks.

"Your jaw still hurting? We can have someone take a look at it if you would like," Detective James says,

"No...thank you." Alice is adamant. Since arriving at the police station, she refuses to speak to anyone and doesn't allow anyone to touch her.

She has no recollection of who she is and how she got to where she had been found. She had woken up a few hours ago to discover that she was covered in blood. The worst part is that the blood is not hers. There is no sign of a struggle according to detective James. Alice tries several times to remember who she is and how she wandered to the middle of nowhere, but no matter how hard she tries, nothing comes to mind.

"Alight...so, what did you want to tell me?" Detective James asks,

"When can I leave?" Alice asks,

"About that...it is not possible until we find out what happened to you and whose blood you had on you," Detective James responds,

Alice already expects as much. "I already told you. I do not-"

"I believe you...really, I do. It's just that..." he looks at the window behind him. He knows his boss is standing in the other room watching the interrogation.

"Can I have something to eat? Please? I would really like to get some sleep," Alice says after a few seconds of silence.

"Uhm…" detective James hesitates for a few seconds agreeing to her request.

"Thank you," Alice says,

×××

In her cell, the pain in her lower back gum is near unbearable for her. Alice feels around with her fingers the area where her gum aches.

"Hmmm?" Alice feels a weird object where her molars are meant to be. She walks to the mirror and looks through the mirror. It looks like a metal filling, but the only difference is, it is weirdly shaped. Putting her hands around the object which appears to be lodged in her tooth, Alice feels the object move slightly.

"What the…" she curves her finger and uses her nail to pull out the object.

There is a tiny button on the metal device. Alice looks around to make sure no one sees her. She presses the button which immediately causes a faint red light to blink randomly. She holds the device in her hands for a while, but apart from the blinking light, there is nothing else that happens.

Alice, just as she is about to throw the device away, hears a faint noise coming from the device.

"Hmm?" She puts the device close to her ears.

"Alice…can you hear me?" A woman's voice can be heard coming from the device. Alice is startled. However, there is something about the woman's voice that makes her feel she could trust the woman.

"Who is this?" Alice asks,

"Oh, thank god! Listen to me, Alice. I know you have no recollection of who you are and how you got yourself into this mess. It was not my idea, it was your idea…" the woman speaks quickly. Alice has no time to process the fact that she has something to do with her predicament.

"Listen, your memories are temporarily blocked. The effects of the drug should wear out in an hour. When it does, you will remember and know exactly what's happening and why you're there. Good luck. Oh! Check the reflection of the tattoo."

As Alice is about to speak and ask who she's speaking to, the voice disappears,

"Hello? Hello?" Alice is distraught. The one person who could tell her what is happening has disappeared from her.

However, her dismay soon fades as she remembers the words of the woman. In an hour, she will have her memories back. Alice is hopeful. At this point, she has a lot more questions than she had before. Especially when she realizes that her present dilemma was her plan. Why would she do this to herself? Alice is desperate to know.

Alice lays on one of the prison beds in silence as she watches the clock tick. She has no idea what drug was capable of blocking her memories and bringing them in such a timely fashion.

As she watches the clock tick 15 minutes till an hour, Alice feels an immense pain assail her. She grabs onto her head as she tries her best not to scream. She feels as though her head is about to explode.

As she rolls on the bed, flashes of images begin to play out in her head. The answers to the questions she was desperately seeking begin to rush in waves.

This lasts for five minutes, but these five minutes feel like hours. She can barely hold on.

"Alice?" Detective James walks up to the cell. "It's time. I have a few more questions for you."

Alice feels the pain subside drastically. She turns around and looks at detective James. However, unlike the way she looked at him earlier, her look holds immense hatred and anger at the man in front of her. She wants nothing more than to strangle him to death.

"Right." Alice tries her best not to expose herself.

The interrogation is no different. Alice keeps up with the act of not remembering anything. However, unlike before, it is significantly harder. Detective James also notices that something is off about the woman seated across from him, but he cannot put his finger on it.

Alone in the interrogation room, Alice looks at the clock on the wall. She is expectant.

"Alice?" The familiar voice drifts into her ears as she stares at the wall clock.

"Moira?" Alice responds with a wide smile on her face.

"You're back! Oh, thank goodness…I was getting worried." Alice can hear the excitement in the woman's voice.

"Is everyone ready?" Alice asks,

"Yes. We are good to go," Moira responds,

"Good! It is high time these people pay for what they did to Dan." Alice clenches her fist in anger.

"When you create the distraction, I'll escape and look for the documents being kept in the storeroom. We have to expose them," Alice says,

"I know…and we will," Moira responds,

"Dad would be proud of us." Moira's voice is soft but it carries with it, a lot of emotion.

"He would," Alice responds,

"It's time. Go ahead!" Alice speaks up as soon as she sees the clock strike at 7 pm.

Alice immediately coils into a ball and tries her best to relax her body as much as possible. As soon as she does, an explosion rocks the entire building.

<boom>

Underneath the building, there seems to be a huge lab. Alice can see several people dressed in white running away as parts of the building begin to collapse. To her shock, she sees several bodies being harvested.

"I was right," Alice says through gritted teeth.

"Alice! Mark and the others are on their way," Moira's voice snaps Alice from her thoughts.

"Alice? Alice…are you there?"

HER

Today makes it eight months since I lost my husband and I really can't explain why I killed him. Was it because he cheated? No. I forgave him twice for that.

Well, not really what you'd call forgiveness per se, but I accepted his plea and decided to move on.

I went on performing my duties as his wife after his *mistakes* even though deep down, I had resisted the urge to strangle him in his sleep for the past 2 years.

I never did move on.

Brian was a real scum and even though I can't explain why I killed him, at least I can explain why I should have killed him long ago.

24th of October 2012 was the date.

I call thrice to inform him of my homecoming, but he doesn't pick up, which is strange. Brian always picked up his phone even while sleeping. At this point, I am slightly worried, but I hate myself for it when I get home.

At this point, he isn't expecting me until Saturday, but I have to leave the business trip early as things aren't going as planned. If only I knew, I wouldn't have gone home. I would have stopped at a hotel and spent the night or worse, just sit there, anywhere. Anywhere I went that day would have been better than going home but I was so excited to see my husband and grin satisfyingly when I see the look on his face and his dimpled smile upon my arrival. Everything is planned in my head. *All he has to do is follow the script,* I think but little do I know that I am the one about to be surprised.

The door is unlocked so I let myself in and there it is, the sight, the horrible sight that keeps repeating in my head every single night! The sight of Brian and his cousin! Who the hell has sex with their cousin? At this point, the smile on my face has vanished already and my blood is boiling.

I don't know which would be faster to get hold of, the knife in the kitchen, the pieces of metal in the garage, or would my heels do? *I just want to taste the blood of this lunatic.*

I mean, yes. With what the world has become today, I can't answer the question of whether it is or not bad to marry your cousin or your stepsister. But come on, you don't need an Einstein to confirm to you that having sex with your cousin outside marriage is an obnoxious and morally despicable act, to say the least.

Trust me, Noah will be pissed he didn't miss the boat if the news gets to him.

I have never liked Sapphira (Brian's cousin) slightly because she reminds me of the Sapphira in the holy bible. I know that's an unreasonable reason to hate someone, but I just have this gut feeling about her and I need to link it to something 'cos trust me, it is horrible to just hate someone without reason(s). Now seeing her half-clothed with my husband in my home, on my couch (God! They couldn't even get a proper room) justifies the hate. You know that feeling when you think someone was shit and they did prove they were shit? I couldn't believe I was right!

At this point, she can't raise her head as she passes by me at the door, and trust me, there and then, I want to grab and pull her hair out strand by strand and just punch her in the face. Punch her in the face till she stops breathing but she isn't my husband and I strongly believe a good partner shouldn't cheat no matter how powerful the seduction might be so, I let her go.

I face my husband who is now sitting, putting on his clothes and I am so enraged by how calm he looks that I can't wait any longer. The silence is killing me.

"You won't say anything?" I break the silence.

"Babe I..." he begins to say but I cut him off mid-sentence.

"Don't. Don't babe me!"

He sighs and then he resumes.

"Natalie, I don't think there's something to say."

Lord, give me strength. The way he is talking unapologetically makes me want to cut him into two and take out his internal organs, but I doubt it's time for that yet.

"I'll tell you what, I do have something to say. Brian, you couldn't wait two days without having sex? Two fuckin' days? What if I was going for a week? Or say a month? What would you do then, huh? I guess you would invite all the hoes in the area and have a fuckin' orgy party!"

"Do you know what you are? I'll tell you what you are. You are a loose and sexually disoriented son of a bitch!"

I know Brian doesn't like talking about his parents or his past. He hates hearing about it, but I am too livid to stop here so I add:

"I wonder if your mum ever taught you about sex education or let me guess, you probably called in sick the day you were being taught in school 'cos WTF!"

Our gaze meets and I see him discreetly wipe away a tear, but I am too cold at that moment to give a shit.

I just made a grown man weep and I'm loving it but little do I know that my "moment of victory" is about to be squashed.

"I want a divorce," he says.

Upon hearing this, I almost fall to the ground. This man is undoubtedly crazy.

"You what?"

"You heard me. I said I want a divorce," he repeats. This time, he even cleared his throat.

The nerve. Jesus, it is the nerve for me.

"You definitely are crazy. I just caught you doing the unthinkable with your cousin and now you want a divorce? If anybody wants a divorce in this marriage, it should be me. Am I a joke to you? Where's this coming from? Since when you have been nursing the thought?" I reply angrily.

What he says next will go down in history as one of the top ten worst reasons for wanting a divorce.

"For some time now, I have been feeling like I am not wanted in this marriage anymore, and honestly, I want to be where I am wanted, where I can be happy."

I laugh at this, a loud wicked laugh.

Look who is playing the victim! I used to believe happiness is for everyone. But after cheating on me several times, I disagree that this *cousin fucker* deserves happiness.

"I feel like I am not wanted in this marriage anymore," I repeat, mockingly.

"And who're you going to marry then? Tell me, who's going to supply you with the happiness you seek? Sapphira? Melissa? Or... Oh, is there a new one in town?"

"I don't think that's any of your business," he replies, his face looking away.

"Ooooh, looks like you have it all planned out. Please yourself then," I say with a wry smile before making my way to the bedroom.

And looking back to that day, I blame myself. I regret not ending it there. Why didn't I kill him that day? The reason, I'll never know.

×××

The prison cell is barely six feet by four. The walls are the same thick gray stone as the dwellings of the region, but instead of a wide window with a flower box, there is a mean barred opening with thick metal bars and no glass.

In the summer, the fresher air is a relief, helping to alleviate the stench of festering sewage but in the cold seasons, it lets in a wicked draft and reduces the temperature to near freezing. It is no brighter inside than the gathering gloom of dusk, even at midday.

The bed is a wooden board on legs. There is no mattress, no cushioning, and only one thin blanket. It is either suffocating quietly or pierced with the screams of tortured inmates.

You can say I deserve it and maybe I do. I was sleeping with a married man and look where it got me.

I just wanted to tell him I will keep the baby. I just wanted to shout at him for rejecting the pregnancy then leaving. I never thought I will be provoked to that extent... To the extent of hitting him on the head with a vase, repeatedly before shooting him twice with the gun in his cabinet, his damn gun! However, could you blame me?

He called me a hoe. The bastard called me a hoe! I did everything to satisfy him.

He told me he wasn't happy in his marriage and I gave him happiness (or thought I did).

I didn't know I was just one of his 'time passers'. He promised we would be married and be together, but he lied!

He looked into my eyes and lied, just like all men do.

×××

I am not sure what I'm feeling. Is it anger? Pain? Sadness? These feelings are so intertwined that perhaps their names ought to be tweaked to reflect their true origins.

I loved Brian till the end and it gives me joy to see him in his dying moments, struggling to live.

Isn't this what they mean when they say, "Till death do us part?" I guess I can be proud of fulfilling at least one of my marriage vows.

He looks so innocent in his dying moment; you'll think he has never committed a single error in his life. I watch coolly as he drags himself on the floor in search of his phone which, at that time, was securely in my fully gloved hand and I must say, the way he gasps for breath turns me on.

I had brought my colt m1911 pistol with a silencer I got on eBay but seeing as he's already struggling to live, guess I won't be needing it anymore. Maybe I am not the only one that wants this son of a bitch dead after all.

From the look of things, the potential killer is probably a female as the person didn't check if the job was done and it appears whoever it was, she left in a hurry.

Why am I here trying to play Sherlock Holmes when instead, I should be playing Aileen Wuornos or Villanelle or any female that has ever wielded a gun and killed a man?

He has now reached what I'll call his breaking point. The gasps are reducing and since I didn't bring my pistol for auctioning coupled with the fact that I'll like to kill this guy myself, I shoot him in the chest, very close to where he was initially shot.

"I love you, Brian," are the words that come out of my mouth.

Did I kill him? You could say so.

But he was dying when I got here and would probably die even if I hadn't shown up but either way, I couldn't have been happier to pull the "deciding trigger" and speed up the whole process.

×××

In other news, Police have reopened an investigation involving the murder of Brian stones. He is 32 years of age at the time of his death and is killed on the afternoon of Monday, 27th of August.

Investigations were previously closed due to the last of substantial evidence(s) leading to a narrow lead but in a recent interview, the detective in charge of the case, inspector Rowland Jarvis says in a quote: "There is now a fresh lead and an ironic twist of events which could change the whole outlook of the case."

He also adds that the general public should remain calm and collected as the police are doing everything in their power to investigate properly, close in on every lead, and bring the killer to justice. He assures an honest and open update in case anything comes up which the public should know about.

And lastly, he adds, "But for all these to happen, we must be allowed to do our jobs."

Natalie drops the remote upon hearing this. A fresh lead? An ironic twist of event? She made sure she didn't leave anything behind; her alibi is solid as hell, and she wasn't too emotional when investigated.

What was it that she did wrong? What didn't she say?

She runs inside to check the coat she wore that day and that is when she notices something, something so trivial…

The sixth and last button on her coat isn't there anymore.

"Shit!"

THE SIX

It all begins on a typical day, as I am walking down the street.

A man in his 50's, with rough beards and a rough face, who is living a rough life is calling after me. "Wait! Wait!" I look back to be sure of what is happening, then I begin to walk faster, picking up pace, but he isn't sopping either. *Did I drop something? Definitely not,* I think.

I start running now since walking fast isn't cutting it, but before I can run 3 feet forward, he catches up with me and holds my hand. I struggle to let go, but he is obviously stronger.

"Itzel, don't shout, don't panic."

"How... how did you know my name?" That reply is born out of a tired and frightened mind because my breathing is now irregular. God! I'm out of shape.

"Forget about that and listen to me closely. What I'm about to tell you is very important, and your life depends on it." He pauses for a moment as passersby's are beginning to stare.

I want to scream for help at that moment, but this man knows my name. *What if he just guessed?* I wonder. Honestly, no. Who would have guessed that your name is "Itzel" when there are lots of other options to guess from. Like Jessica, Sarah, Karen, and the likes.

This man knows me, and I should listen to him out.

He lets go of my hand now, and I massage my wrist.

"In the next few days or weeks even, you're gonna receive some messages. Very critical and arcane. Do well to ignore these messages and definitely resist the urge to contact the numbers."

Ugh, this man is starting to sound like my dad, and I'm not too fond of it.

"Oh, look. It's the stranger giving instructions for me to ignore strangers; how ironic! Do you have a manual on this? I want to get one."

"This is not a joke, Itzel!" He raises his voice before realizing he shouldn't have.

"Look, I'm sorry, but you have to understand the urgency of the situation. These guys are..."

"Which guys?" I interrupt.

"You can't really know them. They are functioning but do not exist. They don't have a place, but they are everywhere, and once you interest them, they'll find you."

"At least I interest some people," I reply sarcastically.

"Are you even listening?"

"So... How did you know about them? Are you something like their runaway agent or something?"

"I have been studying their pattern for some time, and I have found that you are the next one that they will pick."

"Interesting... So, what do they like... to do to their picks?"

"You wouldn't like it, trust me."

"Oh, you have no idea what I like."

"Stop trying to be acerbic, Itzel. These guys are not planning to take you on a vacation in Hawaii, and they certainly don't give a damn about buying you expensive skincare products. These people will zap the joy out of your life, and there's nothing you will be able to do about it."

"So... They're like my exes then, brilliant."

Upon hearing this, the stranger shakes his head in disappointment. I'm sure at that very moment, he wondered why I had been picked.

"What is your name then?" I ask.

"It is better if you don't know."

"But you know mine."

"Trust me. It is for your own good."

"For my own good? A stranger with weird-looking features has stopped me and he knows my name and tells me about a freaking set of non-existent people but guess what? He won't tell me his goddamn name!"

"Knowing my name won't change anything, Itzel."

"Okay then. Have a nice life, and don't even dare stop me anywhere again 'cos God knows, I'm calling the cops on you!" After saying this, I start walking away from him; then I hear him say almost inaudibly, "The six."

I look back, "What?"

"That's what I call them, *the six*."

×××

Tyler is just staring and twisting the copper ring around his fingers. In the summer sunlight, it shines in a way that is too brown to be gold but too golden to be bronze. It wraps around his fingers like licorice.

His wife has just died and standing there, I can see he is drained of strength and hope. Looking up to the watery skies and heaven beyond, he has to believe his wife is safe up there, comfortable, and warm because to look down is to imagine her cold in a box, bereft of his cuddles and goodnight kisses.

You can feel it in this funeral that the good people that die leave in us a part of their goodness because everyone present here feels that need to reach out and absorb it once more, that memory that keeps our soul sparks burning bright.

After the "May her soul rests in perfect peace and thanks for coming," I decide to wander around the cemetery a little.

I have always believed that tombstones mark the passing of one who'd been so beloved, who'd left behind the kind of legacy that made the world a better place, and reading the messages on these people's tombstones, I couldn't agree more.

I continue walking and reading when suddenly, something catches my eye.

Upon the neatly kept grass, upon the stretching green sat one tombstone identical to its peers. Yet this one brings upon me the greatest flood of fear and dread, for the name etched upon it, is like mine or wait, is mine. The date of birth is of no difference either. Only something is missing, the date of death; the column is left blank.

My heart sinks.

xxx

I wake as if it's an emergency as if sleeping has become a dangerous thing. My heart beats fast, and there is a buzzing in my head, and together, they are as panic with jump-leads. My brain is like a flat battery, still recovering from yesterday's hangover, drinking, and nightmares.

I reluctantly drag myself out of bed to get a cup of water, and that is when I notice my phone light up with texts; I sit back on the bed.

(Unknown sender): Had a good time yesterday.

(Beth): Where have you been?

(Mum): Did you get drunk again?

I ignore the messages and loads of voicemail before coming across a particular one that reads:

(Unknown sender): Blood is really warm; it's like drinking hot chocolate but with more screaming.

I fling my phone across the room and start shaking; I am overwhelmed with fear.

Are the words of the stranger coming to pass already? Am I being contacted by the six? What do they want? I wonder.

The stream of questions keeps flowing nonstop in my head, but the saddest thing is that there is no answer coming forth, and at that moment, there is only one way to know the answers, just one.

I'll have to reply to them. Yeah, I know. Someone warned me against replying to them, but how do I know if his words are true?

Life is a risk. In fact, living is a risk, and without taking risks, you'll end up with lots of *what-ifs* after all is said and done.

Come to think of it, what if 'the six' are a bunch of government officials choosing people at random and making them rich? Or Royal families seeking a bride for their prince and sending coded messages?

It doesn't make a lot of sense, but you can't rule out the possibility, and that's it with life, you can't rule out options, and you never know. You never know unless you walk into it.

I walk to where my phone is lying on the ground, pick it up, and get ready to send a reply.

A part of me want to dial 911, but I don't want to spoil the fun. I need to get to the bottom of this. If these guys truly exist, I need to know who they were and what they are on about.

My hands are trembling as I type the words 'who are you?' I wait for some seconds to confirm that I am sane and making the right decision before hitting the send button.

I have barely sent it when a message enters, probably automated (I think), and the content is... I don't know, kinda normal? Like you've just subscribed for a package unless, I don't know what I subscribed for, the message reads:

'Thanks for joining our subscriber list!'

That's it? I think to myself before walking in the bathroom and going on with my normal activities.

But only if I had known, I wouldn't have clicked the button. I would have heeded to the stranger's words because what would follow was more, much more than I subscribed for.

×××

It's funny, I did warn her, you know. But I think there's that part of the brain that tells you to go on, dig a little deeper, and it all exists in us. That 'you won't know if you don't go' mentality, that curiosity. We all have it, but the only difference is how we control it.

I know a part of her wanted to ignore or perhaps call for help when she saw the message, but she just couldn't. She is in now. She was in before we even sent the text, preconscious. And that is the main reason why we walk up to them before contacting them, we give them a 'heads up' before throwing the bait, and that's because we know that the human brain never forgets.

We try to stimulate them, ignite their interests, stir up their curiosity. In the long run, they'd think we were doing them a favor by coming to warn them, they'd look back and blame themselves eventually for their 'disobedience,' but it was all part of the plan.

They wouldn't have guessed. I mean, who would have thought you would become a victim just by replying to a text? No one.

We chose females because life is a matter of good and bad for them, or… a phase of black and white. They are just too innocent to understand the real workings, the inner sphere of how life works. Life is more than just being good or being bad. Have they ever considered being good and bad? Yes, being both simultaneously and or being white in black or vice versa.

You can't blame us; you really can't.

We warned them; they didn't listen (even though we know they won't). And here they are, seated, tied up like rams about to be slaughtered and blindfolded.

We have targeted the right ones; we chose them carefully.

Six ladies with no hope. Six ladies they'll stop looking for after maybe a day or two. They are just here to exist; they weren't exactly living.

Of course, we are off the grid. Far off the grid and we have the support of a top government official. We are untraceable, but we do exist.

×××

Sixth in a row

Residents fear for their lives

by Dorville C.

It wasn't the usual bustling town it used to be as the serial kidnapper (whose name and identity are still unknown) strikes again.

According to her neighbor, the latest victim is identified to be 25-year-old Itzel Jackson who was last seen on her way to work on Monday morning.

Daisy Miller, the owner of a coffee shop down her street, raised the alarm on Thursday morning, having not seen her since Monday morning, which was 'very unusual,' quoting him:

"Itzel wouldn't go a day without having a cup of coffee here, I haven't seen her since Monday morning, which was unusual, and that was why I alerted the police. She was free with everyone and easy to relate to. All the workers here like her."

The police are working on it and urge anyone with information regarding any unusual activity on that day or any other day to come forward.

Residents are beginning to panic as this is the sixth person to be kidnapped in 2 months, all women.

They think there's a scheme going on and plead with the police to put in more effort as no one knows who is next.

HYPOTHETICALLY SPEAKING

"911, what's your emergency?"

"I... set my house on fire and I think my parents are dead."

It's something you can't get used to, no matter how many cases you have handled. The smell of smoke emanating from the burning house laced with the ashes of the dead. I take out yet another cigarette that I swear would be my last as I stand in the middle of the chaos around me.

Arson, I'm not sure who I should pity, the 13-year-old kid whose life is going to be ruined forever or his now peaceful parents who no longer have to care for such a troubled child.

"Detective, strange seeing you here," says one of the police officers.

"It is, isn't it? I heard the 911 call and I just had to check it out for myself."

"Well, it's not one of those cases where your Sherlock Holmes skills will be needed. It's a closed case now. We have the culprit who confessed to intentionally burning the house to kill his parents so…"

"True, though everything is not always as it seems in our line of work. You should do well to remember that."

"Sleep easy this night, Detective Trevor. We have this one handled."

A gust of wind sends a chill down my spine as I turn to look at the child murderer. It is like déjà vu. I can't remember what year that case was but this child staring right back at me with eyes that don't match that of a cold-blooded killer looks like the replica of the child that burnt down his foster home. It could just be my imagination, a mere coincidence at best… or my intuition telling me that there is some connection between this case and that one.

×××

I am already tired of what is to come. I almost don't want to enter the house I call home. I know she is going to let me hear it this night. Another night of coming home late. I guess I should be used to her rants by now.

I let out a large sigh as I mentally prepare myself before I open the door.

"Welcome honey, your food is in the microwave," my wife says with the calmest tone.

I'm not sure if I should be relieved or worried.

"Baby, I know I came home late this night again. I'm really sorry. There was a 911 call I couldn't ignore and I ha-"

"I didn't ask for an explanation this time and the one you should be apologizing to is Mia… she waited up for you again. For heaven's sake, Trevor! It's a school night and she is 10! The least you could have done was to call the house and put her to bed. Do you care for her at all?!"

"I'm sor-"

"Don't bother; your apology doesn't mean anything anymore."

I wrap my hands around her waist and kiss her cheek softly.

"I'm getting tired of this, Trevor… it's too much."

"I know baby, I know."

×××

"Your honor, this boy is a child. He has had issues with his mental health in the past; it is clear that he wasn't in his right mind when he started the fire," says the defense attorney.

"I set the fire to kill my parents," the kid blurts out.

"Defense attorney, your client has just made this easy for us," says the judge.

The gavel hits the hardwood causing any chatter echoing through the courtroom to quickly cease.

"The court rules and finds the defendant guilty to the charge of second-degree arson. He is therefore sentenced to three-year incarceration."

"A sad case, isn't it?" A voice from beside me asks.

"Sorry, I'm Doctor Abdul, nice to meet you," he says with his outstretched hand.

"Detective Trevor," I respond accepting his handshake.

"If I may be so bold, what is a detective like you doing at a court hearing, sitting at the back row? Are you a friend of the boy's family?"

"No, I'm not. I'm just an interested party. What about you, doctor?"

"The boy was once my patient. It's sad to see what has become of him. He wasn't the violent type; he just had trouble fitting in. I fear I have failed him as his former therapist," Abdul remorsefully utters.

"I guess you never really know what a person is capable of," I say in response.

"It was nice meeting you, detective."

"Something tells me this would not be our last encounter."

"I guess only time will tell."

This persistent feeling keeps bugging my mind as I look to take one last look at the boy. For someone who just got a three-year sentence, he seems rather calm, almost like his mind is not here but here at the same time.

×××

Three weeks have gone by since the court hearing. I walk into the precinct; the usual chatter fills my ears but the sour expression on my partner's face as she walks towards me drowns out all the noise.

"It's a 13-year-old boy, reported to have stabbed his parents in their sleep," Alice says.

"How was this known?"

"The neighbors called, they said they found him on their front porch with a knife in his hand and him repeating that he killed his parents over and over again."

"Gosh! This just ruins my lunch plans and my wife made a turkey."

"Focus, Trevor. We have to go."

We arrive at the crime scene, just as they are putting the bodies away with their eyeballs nowhere near where they are supposed to be.

"Jesus Christ! A kid did that?"

"Apparently. Our guys are still having trouble trying to get him off the porch and into the car," Alice responds.

I make my way over to the porch to be met with yet another teenage killer but there is nothing. His eyes don't hold any markings of a cold-blooded killer. He looks rather terrified if anything. They finally get him into the car and that's when it hits me.

"Hey, Alice, doesn't this kid remind you of that arson kid that set his house on fire?"

"I guess; they are both around the same age. Come to think of it, they do actually look alike. Why? Do you think there is some connection here?"

"It's just a hunch, for now, nothing concrete yet. Do me a favor and contact me if anything out of normal happens with that arson kid."

"Umm... okay. I will ask my friend down at the center for any new information." We enter the neighbor's house for routine questioning. It doesn't take long before the case is closed and the kid is incarcerated.

×××

"Honey, I'm home!" I yell while struggling to shut the door with a giant teddy bear in my hand.

"You're early," announces my very stunned wife.

"And I come bearing gifts. I said I would be better, didn't I?... This is the first step."

I hear little footsteps from the stairs and soon after, an excited Mia comes jumping on me. It doesn't take long till we both hit the ground laughing. I have missed this.

"This is for you, sweetheart," I say handing her the oversized teddy bear.

"I was about to make dinner, mind helping out like you used to?"

My phone starts ringing. "Just give me one second, babe. I need to take this call."

"Alice, what is it? Now is not a good time."

"Well, you said to get in touch if anything weird happens to that kid, remember?"

"Go on then."

"So, it turns out that he committed suicide a week after his sentence. Poor kid must have been overcome by guilt."

"Or something else. Can you meet me at the precinct in like thirty minutes?"

"Sure why?"

"There is something I need to find out. If you get there before me, pull out all arson cases in the past three years, specifically about children that burnt down family homes... There is something more to this, I just know it."

I hang up the phone and try to comport myself before entering the kitchen and ruining dinner.

"Babe, I'm really sorry but something came up and I have to head back to the office."

She slams the oven shut and turns to me.

"I'm taking Mia with me to my dad's house... I can't keep going on the same rollercoaster with you."

"Baby please, don't do this to me," I plead with her.

"You promised me this wouldn't happen again, but your work has become your obsession once again! You're hardly at home and even when you're here, you always seem very far away... I'm done, Trevor, and I mean it this time."

"Don't come looking for us and don't call!" she yells as she goes upstairs.

Words can't describe the hole that has nestled its way into my heart. My whole world is walking away from me and the saddest part is that I know it's only for the best.

xxx

I return to the precinct with just one thought in my head.

"Alice, did you find anything?"

"Yeah actually, there was one case where some kid burnt down his foster home. It's the strangest thing; he looks like that Shawn kid that killed himself and that's not all. It turns out that this Spencer kid was reported to have committed suicide just three days into his sentencing."

"It's too much of a coincidence. The boy that stabbed his parents, what is his name again?"

"Seth Sage; why?"

"So, these three children freakishly look alike. I mean, even their jawline looks similar. We know their names all start with an S, and we also know that they all killed their parents but what or who links them all together?"

"It's getting pretty late, Trevor; I need to head home. You're not going to let this go, are you?"

"There is something here. I just know it. Both Seth and Spencer looked like they weren't in control of their actions."

"No sane person kills people."

"It's more than that."

Alice leaves the office and I am left struggling with this feeling. I check their medical records. It turns out that they were all treated in the same hospital. The doctor that signed off on their sound mind was Doctor Abdul. Where have I heard that name before? Oh no! Could it be that there were somehow brainwashed into those killings and then overcome by guilt that they committed suicide? What could be his motive? I need to tell the captain about this.

×××

"You come into my office and ask for a search warrant all based on a hunch? Listen, Trevor, while I do admire your dedication to justice, we need hard evidence to build a case on this."

"You know me. I wouldn't be adamant about something if I didn't think there was something here; just look at the kids. They have the same physical features, even down to the jawline structure."

"You always say, if the same thing happens twice, it's a coincidence but if it happens three times, it becomes a pattern. This is a freaking series! These boys are somehow being manipulated into doing these things. I just know it! And who do they all have in common…"

"I'm begging you to drop this. This doctor has connections that can ruin you and put me out of work. For both our sakes, just drop it. Think about your family. It's just not worth it."

I step out of the captain's office. I can't just let this go. I drive to the same hospital to confront him.

×××

"Doctor, I'm detective Trevor. We met at a court hearing?"

"Ah, yes I remember. What can I help you with?"

"How about a quick chat?"

"Am I in any trouble, detective?"

"No, I just wanted to run something by you. By the way, I notice you have mostly male patients."

"Yes, I have a particular interest in male children."

"Hypothetically speaking, is it possible to hypnotize someone into killing his parents? If yes, why would the person use hypnosis? I can't possibly think of the motive behind that."

"Hypothetically speaking, it is very much possible to hypnotize someone into killing just about anybody. For the motive, it could be that the person just wanted to have said killer all to himself and saw the parents as mere obstacles that needed to be removed. Then again, it all depends on perspective."

A BUTCHER'S DIARY

I am just like any other person you meet in your everyday life. I like to live, love, play game, hang out, and I like to kill, just like everyone else. The difference is some hunt lions, tigers, deer, or elks. As for me, I like to hunt the most dangerous predator, humans.

I never get to share my thoughts with anyone, mostly because they'll judge me. Other people won't understand me. And if someone does find out about my little hobby, they end up somewhere out there, drained out of life. So, I have decided to write this memoir of mine- if that's what you want to call it- but at least this way, I will be able to write down my thoughts and daily events.

I have been thinking a lot about going on another hunting trip. Each hunt usually takes up a lot of time and effort, to say the least. Consider it like painting your masterpiece. First, I would need a paintbrush, and I would have to buy new equipment.

I go to the farthest hardware store. I don't let myself get too distracted with all the other 'toys' there. So I gather what supplies I will need and head for the checkout counter. The girl on the other side of the counter is a fine-looking woman; her porcelain skin could be a very nice addition to my collection.

In fact, I have always kept her on my list of potential collections, like adding something to your cart, but the opportunity hasn't been too kind to me. Too bad, she does look extraordinarily flawless this night, as a brand-new shiny toy, but I keep my head in the game.

The girl behind the counter gives me a puzzled look when I approach her with my cart full of a tranquilizer gun, an electric saw, some pliers, and some extra durable ropes.

"You're not a serial killer, are you?" the girl asks me with a teasing smile.

I don't pay any attention to her rhetorical query. I am taken away by the beauty and the perfection of her skin. *I have to have her; she is just too fine of a specimen to let go,* I think.

"Yeah, you'd think that, but no, I am actually going for an expedition in the forest for a few days," I smile and reply to her comment.

I said the truth, just not all of it. I can't exactly say I am going hunting; women nowadays usually don't take hunting very kindly. She smiles and proceeds to check my items.

"You know you are very beautiful," I say.

She smiles and thanks me. I can't hold it much longer. I have to make a move now before she's done checking my items and tells me to leave.

"Listen, before I go on the trip, would you mind going out with me tonight?" I just blabber out the words from my mouth. I am scared as I say it and I am sweating like a pig. My heart starts to race with unfathomable excitement,

She stares at me for almost two whole minutes looking shocked and confused, but most importantly, not repulsed. When she does break the silence, to my relief, she breaks the silence with a smile and looks down to swipe the last of my items, the electric saw on the counter.

"So? Will you?" I ask again, trying to keep her eyes off the cart, now more eager than before.

"I always wondered if you were ever going to ask me out," she smiles bigger now. I am overtaken by sheer joy, so much delight that I can't even put it into words.

"So, 8 pm at my house? It's just up the street, the third building, eight-floor," I ask her.

"I would love to," she smiles back at me, turning slightly red.

I give her my number and head out with my stuff. *It's going to be a good day today.* I can just feel it in my bones. I have never felt this sudden surge of excitement since my last hunt, and even that is nothing compared to this. To be honest, the last hunt was not even as close to being perfect as this one.

I have a lot of work to do back at home before the girl arrives, I have to prepare a special room, prepare the table, and arrange the silverware. I have to work fast to make sure everything is perfect.

Just imagining her precious porcelain skin makes everything worth it. The last Rendezvous I had here left its marks on the walls of the room. It was quite messy. I have to take care of that, too.

Night comes surprisingly quickly as I shift my gaze outside; it is around seven-thirty when the bell rings. I am taken aback as I am so lost in the novella in my hands. Just as the bell rings, I sprint for the door. It is the girl. She looks so amazing in her little red dress. Her skin looks softer than luxurious feathers.

"Can I come in?" she asks sarcastically, seeing that I am at a loss for words seeing her.

"Yes, of course, come in. You look amazing, by the way," I tell her as I let her in.

"Take a seat on the couch, and I'll get some wine." I have seen in my days that it helps to calm them down with some social lubricants, as they say.

"I would love some," she smiles and winks at me. I like it when they are so full of life. It just makes everything more enjoyable.

The wine glasses always have my trusty roofies by their side; you never know when you might need it. I mix some in her glass of wine before serving her.

She seems to fancy me. It looks like she won't mind staying indefinitely. It is okay. She can stay forever.

Her words get more slurry as the roofies are taking effect; she seems to have realized by now that this isn't just some wine-induced drunkenness, but before she can even say anything about it, she just falls on the carpet like a rag doll.

Now my clock starts. I have to take her to my special room and have to prepare her before the roofies wear off, and she starts screaming right here. That would be troublesome.

My special room is my place of comfort and pleasure, my very own man cave, you could say. The padded walls mean not a single sound could go out, and none can get in. I like my privacy. It is the perfect place for me, and I have all my tools lined up neatly on the table on the side of my operating table. That soft, delicate little girl is going to make me feel so good for the years to come; she is going to be one of my most prized possessions. I will take good care of her.

I tie her arms and legs up as strongly as I can on my operating table, but I am careful not to inflict bruises or cuts. I don't like to tie up my prey when I sink into their skin to cut them open to drain their blood and skin them. I like to hear the sounds they make, the screams they produce -- d such wonderful melodies to my ears. I never want to miss out on that. It's the highlight of the hunt.

As I am preparing her, I notice her eyes twitching. She is coming back to consciousness. How delightful! Now we can have real fun. As she slowly wakes up, she looks around herself. I greet her. I don't want to be a rude host, after all. I stand by her head and run one of my hands on her delicate flawless skin.

"Hello, darling, you're finally awake," I greet her with a calm voice.

"Where am I? Why am I tied up? What are you doing to me?" she starts to squirm.

Now, this isn't anything new to me. They always act like this. They just don't understand that they are going to become a part of the most amazing collection of works of art anywhere on the entire planet. They're going to live forever to satisfy my pleasure.

"Sshh, my love, you just enjoy this. I am going to make your stay with me for a long time," I reassure her.

She doesn't seem to like it so much. Instead of calming down and thanking me, she starts to scream such horrendous and hateful words.

"No, you fucking maniac, let me out! Let me out now!" Like everyone else.

I frown, too much stress won't do her skin complexion any good. I know telling her that this was all for our good and to preserve her beauty will help her understand, but I don't have to respond now. I just have to keep doing my work and enjoy her song while I do it.

I start with my favorite tool in the kit, my newly sharpened trusty hunting knife. I can't just dismember her like any other animal I caught; she is a special one, so she needs to be treated with utmost delicacy.

As her beautiful naked body lies bare on the table, I can feel my passion burning, and my whole body feels hot. I need her blood in me. I put my knife on her throat as she screams and begs for my mercy, and there is nothing to have mercy about. She doesn't understand that I am giving her the gift of making her immortal! Oh well, no reason to listen to her hysterical breakdowns now. I have to listen to her song and get a whiff of her flesh.

The bright red light shines on top of us as I slowly dig in the tip of my knife into the skin on her throat. It cuts like butter; the feeling of the knife piercing her skin sends euphoric waves down my spine. Oh, how I missed this delight. Not taking the knife out, I drag it down to her beautiful chest.

This is where she starts singing perfectly, hitting all the right notes, and her song is made of the blood trapped in her throat, which makes a gurgling noise every time she tries to scream. It feels so good to finally hear her sing the song of blood.

I bring some buckets to accommodate so much blood; I place them under the table where the blood is dripping over. Now, I can't spend the entire night listening to her sing. I have work to do, so I proceed to cut open her breasts.

Oh, the joy I feel as I cut them open! My hunting knife cuts them open like a hot knife through butter. It is so satisfying. I can't help myself. I have to have a taste, so I hunch down and have a lick of her blood-soaked breasts. It's a feeling of utter bliss having the taste of her blood for the first time. It tastes exactly how I expected it to, such a precious girl. Her blood is bound to taste this good.

I notice she has stopped singing. She can't be dead just yet! Could she? I do tend to get carried away in times like this. They often just die on me so soon. I don't want her to die right now.

We had a wonderful night I had planned up ahead. I just have to check. I sink my knife a little bit deeper into her throat, a squirt of blood comes out covering my face, and she starts gurgling again. The sound of her scream almost echoes in the room. Such bliss when they cry out like this. It gives me more encouragement than anything.

What I want to do with her is what I always do with my prey; I skin them and use their skin for leather. It's nothing too out of the ordinary for someone to do. We do the same thing with other animals without even paying attention. We, humans, are animals too, you know? You can't blatantly discriminate like that. Shame on you.

After I have cut through from her throat down to her genitals, then comes the part where she stops singing. As much as I enjoyed listening to it, it has to come to an end then. To skin her, I have to dismember her head. I have plans for her head too, and I am going to taxidermy it; I did say I was going to keep her for myself for as long as I live, and I meant it. She is my special person now.

As I approach her head gently intending to cut it off with my trusty hunting knife, I notice she isn't fully dead, but she is going to be in about a few minutes. Her singing has stopped, then the only music I can hear is the blood rushing to come out from her cut arteries and the dripping of blood in my buckets.

Of course, I am not going to wait for her to pass out. What is the fun in that? I just dive right in. I drive the knife into her throat and start thrusting it. Her veins and arteries are splitting open under my knife and my own hands. It is all so satisfying. She still makes some gurgling noises as if she can feel me beheading her. It feels so touching, and I will remain in her memories even after she has lost consciousness. She was such a romantic.

Oh, the blood! The beautiful blood that flows from within her, has spread a beautiful odor of intestines and blood all over the room. I never wear any mask while working on my operating table.

I pity the ones that do. Why miss out on such an amazing pleasure of the senses?

As I dig deeper, I notice the knife is having a hard time cutting through her vocal cords. I have to severe that first, how foolish of me. I was lost in so much fun that I didn't even notice.

Well, no harm done, I think to myself and start chopping on her throat. With the first chop, her vocal cords lead out the last gargle. She lasted a long time; most of them just died within the first few minutes. I like how she was a fighter.

As I chop down on her bits and pieces, the shrapnel of bones and some blood flow towards me. I consider them as my souvenirs. The buckets are almost full at this point, so I bring more to accommodate such an awesome flow of blood.

Eventually, I chop off the last bit of skin and flesh that is left on her neck. Finally, I have her beautiful face with me; she's mine forever and ever. I can't help myself. I have to steal a kiss. I am certain she wouldn't mind. After all, we are going to be spending a lot of time together.

The taste of her lips mixed with her blood gives me an incomparable high. I can't t stop myself from kissing her. She has such good and soft lips that are superbly better now that she is dead. It looks like she likes it when I kissed her as well. She is going to have such a good time here. I just know it.

No, I will make sure of it.

Now I have to work on the body to skin her. I put the head on the side table, and I cut open her wrists, severing her hands. To skin someone, I will advise you to always start from the limbs. They're always the hardest. Always chop their wrists and feet off first, and then cut them from one end to the other. Of course, it's not as easy as I make it sound, but if you enjoy it as much as I do, it's all good. Some of your prey might even get completely damaged trying to do this but never get disheartened, and as I like to say, never give up. There is plenty of prey out there.

As I am cutting up her body, I hear my doorbell ring. *Fuck! This is the last thing I need now, right!* People other than me don't understand this. They always judge me for my passion. But I can't just wait for them to go away. That is suspicious. I go to the door to take a look at who it is. As I peek into the eye hole of the door, I see it is the delivery man. I don't remember ordering something. I have to make sure.

"Who is it?" I ask him, trying not to sound suspicious.

"Here from FedEx with your mail," the boy says. I don't remember ordering something that needs to be delivered at 10 pm.

But I figure, oh well, the more, the merrier.

"Come in, the door's unlocked," I tell him, trying to sound too busy to be able to open the door.

As the boy comes into my apartment to place the package on my table, I close the door behind him. He isn't facing me as I do that.

"Why did you close the doo-" he turns around, asking me, but before he can finish his sentence, he looks my way, and instinctively, he is petrified to see me. I couldn't blame him. I do look horrendous.

Before he can say another word, I slash his throat open, letting the tsunami of blood flow; I take a spoonful taste of it. And it hits me. *Yes, tonight is truly going to be splendid.*

I guess my visit to the campsite will have to wait.

MAYOR

Silva is cruising his beat at an even speed alone. His partner is unavailable for the night, so it is just him in the car.

He rubs his hands together to gather warmth and his hand leaves the wheel in the direction of the door handle where the window dials are when his walkie squeaks, Dispatch is reaching out, so he holds on and listens,

"Possible 10-56 at Lower Manhattan, an apartment building on 16th street. Available units in the area, please respond."

The dispatcher repeats it once more and the radio squeaks back into silence. Silva bends to look outside the windscreen. He is on 15th street. A couple of blocks to the right, and he'll be right on the scene. He grabs the walkie out of its cradle and speaks into it.

"Available unit in the area, responding to 10-56, over."

He puts it back into the cradle and changes gears to be faster. 10-56 is the code for suicide. Suicides are gruesome, especially in summer. Identifying the body, notifying the relatives, processing all the paperwork. So much to do.

When reaching the building, there is a little crowd of people outside in a sort of semi-circle. A phone or two is out, flashlights bright in the night. The car shuts down with a little protest, and Silva opens his door and pokes his head outside. The air is still as cold. *Don't these people have anything better to do? Like sleep?* He blows into his hands and ducks back into the car and calls for extra units.

×××

Mercer looks into the kitchen on his way out. He'll get the coffee in a flask to go on his way out. Coffee is essential to keep him going. Especially with late-night calls like this. He is already awake and showered when he gets the call at 2 AM. He sleeps badly these days. Thirty years on the force would do that to you. A dark T-shirt with gray pants is what he chose to wear. He grabs the coffee and his jacket on the way out and tucks his detective badge into his shirt. As he puts his flask to his mouth, he muses on the call out. It is from his station commander, and it sounds hush-hush. He is asked to double time, but he isn't doing anything of the sort. The body isn't going anywhere. It's too cold and too stiff. Taking one more sip from the flask, he gets into his car and backs out of the driveway.

×××

"Hey, Detective Mercer," the cop at the yellow tape calls out to him while handing him the crime scene log. He says 'hi' to him, scribbles his name on it and hands it back to the man. He looks around a bit; it is 3 AM, and the crowd is on the other side of the street, well kept away. Three cop cars are parked outside the line.

"Your partner is over there with the body. The crime scene techs have already gone to work."

Mercer nods his thanks and ducks under the tape that the officer lifted for him. He goes in the direction of the body. Flashes go off, but this time, it is the professionals handling their business. He stays out of the way and looks at the corpse on the pavement from not too far away. It seems to be a man, and the side of his face that is on the floor is crushed. He can tell from the pieces of membrane showing from under it. The rest of the body is splayed in a very distorted pose. His bones have broken on impact and have arranged themselves according to the angle of his fall. The crime scene techs have not moved the body, which is good. The body, the way it lay and the things around it always tell a story. Mercer folds his arms and comes closer. He sees that rigor mortis hasn't set in yet, so John Doe didn't die immediately. Such a painful way to go. He sighs and lifts his head. His partner is coming towards him, concluding that he is done with his preliminary looking around.

"What's up, Mercer? Find everything to your liking?"

"Yeah. Mostly. Preliminaries."

There is a little silence while they both look at the body.

"Say, Jones," Mercer speaks, "cap called you out, too?"

"Yeah. He did. Why? He called you?"

"Yep. It's the same thing with me. I wonder why? I can hear the dispatcher well enough."

Jones grunts a laugh and tells him that the apartment building is very expensive. The odds of a regular person like him and Mercer buying an apartment here are just about zero. That means that whoever was on the floor has cash to burn, and that makes them important because people tend to come from important families. Hence, why the captain has taken up the job himself.

"We still don't know who he is?" Mercer asks, thoughtfully.

"Naaah. Not yet. Fingerprints are mostly gone, only useless partials, but dentals seem to be alright and they're running it as we speak. We should have an answer before the sun comes up."

"I see. Thanks, Jones."

Jones steps away to give Mercer space to work. He likes to get a feel for the scene without being interrupted. His oxfords squeeze as he squats to look at the body properly. The techs have finished and shrouded the body with a tarp that he slowly eased off. *Who are you, mystery man?* He thinks. *How did you die?* He inclines his head and looks at the balcony on the sixth floor from where John Doe has jumped. Pretty decent distance to say goodbye from. But then, the distance should have done less damage to the body. He stands and takes out his gloves from his jacket and puts them on. He then edges the body a little to the side and checks the hands. There is no bruising on the palms or the front of his hands. The body drops neatly into position as he lets it go. His fingers go into all the pockets of the pants on the body, and he doesn't find anything. He knows it has been done already, but he likes to be thorough. He gives the body a once over again and then stands up finally. The gloves are discarded and Jones comes back around him.

"There's something off about this one, Jones. What do you think?"

Jones looks at him weirdly and speaks,

"I don't think so. The guy jumped off his balcony and bought it. Simple as that."

Mercer nods and is quiet as they enter the building and take the elevator up to the sixth floor. They enter the guy's room and begin to look around.

"Any note?" Mercer asks,

"Not that I've seen so far. I was waiting for you to get here before I came up. Keep looking."

They find the guy's jacket and shoes. Nothing is inside. No identification anywhere either. Jones lifts the reading lamp on the desk and whistles,

"Found it."

With gloves, they pick it up. It is short and the text is in a clear hand and written neatly.

Dear dad,

I'm sorry I have to go. I can't continue here anymore.

Don't feel too bad.

Bye.

Mercer bags the note and turns to Jones, who is waiting.

"Something's not right."

"What? With the note?"

"Yeah, that, but I'm talking about the body. If you tripped and were falling, you'd put your hand out to cushion your fall. You wouldn't even think about it. It's a reflex action."

"And so...?"

Mercer walks out onto the balcony.

"The same would apply to a fall from this height. The hand would be put out and the resulting thing would be bruising, externally, and snapped bones internally." He pauses,

Jones takes it up.

"Big boy down there has got no bruises, and you think that if a scan is done, his wrist bones won't be broken the way they're supposed to."

Below them, the coroner's van comes to pick up the body.

"Absolutely right, Jones. Now we've got to visit the coroner and expedite a toxicology screen."

On the ground floor as soon as they get out of the elevator, a uniformed cop is waiting for them.

"Sirs. The dentals just came in. It's the Mayor's son."

The two detectives pause and look at each other before returning to the officer.

"You sure?" Jones gets out first.

"Positive, Sir. The lab double-checked to prevent any kind of problem."

"Thank you, officer," Mercer says dismissively.

Walking to their respective cars, they both know shit will very soon hit the fan.

×××

At the coroner's, what Mercer said is confirmed. Internally, the hand bones didn't break the way they were supposed to. The tox results haven't come in yet, so they go to a food truck across the street to get tacos and wait.

"Are we still handling it as a suicide?" Jones asks him, mouth semi-full.

"I don't think it is, but until the tox report comes out, I won't be sure."

"What are you looking for in the report? It's not as if the guy was drunk when he offed himself. No alcohol in the room and the stench wasn't on his clothes."

"I know. We'll just wait for the report."

His phone trills when he takes the last bite of his taco. He signals for another one to go, wipes his hands, and picks up his phone.

"Mercer here."

It is the Chief calling and he needs to know how far Mercer has gotten on the case.

"It's a suicide, Sir. As far as we know. Some loose ends I'm waiting to tie up before officially declaring it so, but that's what it is."

"That's good, detective. We don't want any surprises and we'd love to have this thing blow over. Anything shady about the boy?"

"Shady how, Sir?"

"You know what I mean, detective. Anything that would embarrass the mayor. I'm trusting you will handle it most discreetly. Make sure to update me on those loose ends, too. Goodbye."

He hands up and Mercer knows what was implied.

"What did he want?" Jones asks,

"High jingo politics, you know how it is. Protect the Mayor from any kind of backlash."

"Yeah, yeah. We'll see about that."

They go back into the coroner's shop and get the tox result.

There is strychnine on it and it is positive. It has been found in his blood. Mercer is then certain that this is no suicide. The mayor's son has been murdered.

Mercer drives back to the station, a little angry that someone has tried to deceive him. He sends Jones to canvass the neighborhood for witnesses and find out if anyone has seen anything. Slim chance, but it is worth taking. At the station, he goes directly to the chief's office and has to wait because there is a guest with him. He nods to the guy standing at the door waiting for someone and sits in the waiting area and gathers his thoughts on how he is going to break this to the chief. A few minutes into his wait, the chief's door opens, and he rises to quickly replace the guest. The mayor steps out first, followed by the chief. The chief sees him first.

"Aha. Here's the detective I was just telling you about. Detective Mercer, meet the mayor."

The man beams at him and shakes hands somberly, conveying just the right amount of sorrow. Ever the politician.

"Detective Mercer. I hear you're the one in charge of my son's...suicide. Thank you for this and your competency. As your chief has told you, I can do without any surprises."

"About that, Sir. There's something. Your son didn't kill himself. He was murdered." He drops it like this so he can watch the mayor's reaction. It is controlled and un-willing to accept what he heard.

"Murdered, you say? But there was a note. He jumped, detective. Surely you're making a mistake."

"No Sir, I'm not. From now, we're treating it as an open murder investigation. I came up here to update the Chief."

The Chief takes his cue and steps in.

"However, this turns out, Mercer, remember our dis-cussion earlier." He smiles and dismisses him, turning to assure the mayor that all will be taken care of properly.

Mercer leaves to go rendezvous with Jones, noting that the waiting guy at the door is now at the mayor's side, taking instructions.

xxx

That night, they meet at a crowded cafe to update themselves on each other's half of the investigation. Jones looks filled to the brim with the information he can't wait to share, but Mercer goes first.

"Met with the Mayor and Chief. They're still seriously pushing the political angle."

"You know enough to expect that, Mercer. Now listen. My canvassing today was almost fruitless until I met a young student from Paris who lives in an apartment building directly opposite the crime scene. Get this; he's a photography student, and he heard a noise at night and checked to see through his window. Saw a man dragging an inert body to the balcony and pushing it over. The man immediately left, but he managed to take a few pictures."

"Let's have them, Jones."

Jones spreads three

color pictures on the dinner table. One is of the man alone on the balcony after flinging the mayor's son down. The other two are of him turning around and going back inside.

Recognition comes immediately to Mercer and he tells Jones.

"Who is it?"

"I don't know his name, but I know it's getting more complicated than it seems. I saw this guy at the chief's office yesterday."

"You did? What was he doing there?"

"I did, and he was with the mayor. Some sort of assistant or driver."

"Jesus, Mercer!" Jones exclaims, "Are you sure? This is one hell of a loaded gun to go to the Chief with."

"Absolutely positive, Jones. The Chief got a good look at him, too. The only logical path is that he killed the mayor's son at the mayor's request. And that is sick. I can't wait to bring him in and know why."

Jones grabs his coat and drops a twenty-dollar bill on the table.

"Let's go," he says with urgency.

xxx

The next day, the mayor and his henchman are in custody, and they have interrogated the truth out of them. It appears that Junior had found papers linking his father with the Russian human trafficking ring right in the city. Papers that went back up to eight years. He hid the papers at his apartment and confronted his father, threatening to expose him. After he left, the man decided on the one course of action that would take his son's life, a little price to pay. The press get wind of it the next day, and the headlines explicitly detailed the mayor's crimes. The city is stunned.

xxx

Detective Mercer sits in his kitchen, and with a cold bottle of beer in his hand, he is satisfied. He toasts the air to celebrate making sure that the dead rested easy, and criminals, even the high-end ones, get what they had coming.

THE BEYOND

The Oklahoma sun is scorching, and Raul has nowhere to shade and hide from the fiery heat. He is trying to get to DC to see his girlfriend and also trying to see as much of the country as possible. He devises a very thrifty way of doing it. Hitching rides. They work, mostly, and that I how he got here, in Oklahoma.

It is a small town with a lot of shrubbery and wooden roads. The sagging signpost read "Welcome to Pryor Creek. Pop: 10,000" when he passes, the owner of the truck he has been in has to turn in another direction, so he gets off and is calculating the way to the nearest diner in what seems to be a pleasant town. He would kill for some cold soda right now.

Raul is a huge man in his thirties. At 6′1, he is very obvious and stands out in a crowd. His muscles are also well defined, shaped from his brief time in the army before he gets an honorable discharge when he finally wakes from a year-long coma. He was army through and through, although he had shed most of its trappings. His hair is dark and his jaw is set at a crude angle. His clothes are pretty neat, considering he only carries about two other sets of clothes in the bag he hangs over his shoulder. His shoes are where the real business is happening because, in this money-saving expedition of his, he sometimes walks long distances before he finds rides willing to take him a little further.

He rubs his hand on his bare chin and looks around. It is a drab road, and the few minutes he spent there, only one car has driven past. A little town with little need for too much movement. Probably has a history for him to explore. He presumes the creek will be somewhere on the outskirts of town, but it has to exist. *Why add creek to a town's name if there's no creek? Pretty stupid,* he thought. He turns around to start walking till he comes across a diner; some food would go down well too. He has last eaten about twelve hours ago. A cop car suddenly comes around the corner, headed directly for him. He stops in his tracks and wonders if this is how swift the police response in this town is. He isn't wondering why the police are there. He knows. The lone driver that passed identified him as a stranger to the town. They must know each other well enough to be able to pick out strangers that quickly. What he is thinking over is why they needed to put the police on him. He hasn't committed any crime, has he? You will never know with these little towns.

The car stops and one officer gets out of the driver's seat and walks towards him. No partner opens up the passenger door to look at him or coordinate with his partner. The police force in the town is considerably small. He takes a deep breath and tries to look as non-menacing as possible. He doesn't want any trouble while he is here. Two days at most to look around and probably find that creek, and then he is out.

"Help you, Sir?" The cop stars. He is a beefy man and his belt barely makes it around his gut.

"Yes, as a matter of fact, I think you could. I'm new in town, and I'd like to find a diner and a motel. One to eat, and the other to shower and sleep."

"And how long do you intend to be with us, Mr...?"

"Mr. Raul, officer. I don't know yet. Maybe a couple of days."

The officer looks at him quizzically for a few seconds, then resumes questioning him.

"Look, Mr. Raul. What's your business here? Tell me, and maybe I could help you hasten it so you'd be on your way, out of our little town."

Raul looks at the man, a little enraged. He has barely even gotten lunch in and they already assembled to throw him out.

"You'd like to run me out, wouldn't you?" He asked, maintaining a level gaze with the cop. "Well, I'm sightseeing, and it will take as long as it needs to be seen. This is America, am I right?"

The cop appears a little stymied but gathered himself.

"Alright, Mr. Raul. I'll drop you off at the local diner. A few streets away from it, you should find a motel. But I'd really like for you to be gone by tomorrow. Get in the car."

Is this guy going to chauffeur him to a diner just like that? After being in such a hurry to throw him out? Well, he doesn't mind in the least, and so he gets in.

The cop turns a couple of streets, and Raul decides to strike a conversation.

"What's your name, officer? I don't see your name tag."

"It's Tooley Duncan and quit asking questions," he answers without even glancing in Raul's direction. They get to the diner's lot and Raul can see from the giant glass windows that it is not full. More like almost empty. He makes his way to get out of the car when the cop clears his throat and speaks again.

"Raul, or whatever your name is, I don't want no trouble in my town, you hear? Don't start anything here.

Peace lovin' folks are all you see here." He gestures in the direction of the diner.

Raul gives him a mock salute and gets out. He stretches in the lot before walking briskly to the diner. The door chimes as he opens it, and the three patrons in it turn to look at him. Their eyes linger for more than what he presumes normal, and then they go back to their food and business. He walks to a table that he calculated can afford him a sole view of the diner's exits and have his back to the wall. It was his habit and it had served him well. The waiter, a young woman of about twenty-four, makes her way to him. He orders steak and a hamburger with soda. She brings him a glass of water with ice, and he says his thanks and gulps most of it down. He sets the glass on the table, refreshed, and looks around the restaurant. It is old, and the Formica on the table is frayed. Probably handed down to several owners over the years. The current owners tried to salvage it by renovating just the little their purses could get away with, but it hadn't done them much good. Raul looks at the other customers apart from him. They are older couples. No young person is in here, and he wonders why. He asks the waitress when she comes with his food.

"Oh. Most people work at the metal plant just close to the outskirts of town. Lunch hour has been over by two hours and you missed them."

"The entire town, at the plant?"

"Yeah, she replies, The Duncans own it and are kind enough to supply the town with jobs. Good people," she says while staring at him and clearly not meaning it.

"The Duncans. Is there an officer that is part of that family?"

"Officer Tooley?" she asks,

"Yeah, that one."

She shakes her head and tells him that even though the Duncans own the plant, they are rarely seen in the town and that it is managed by an external agency.

"They live on the side of the town opposite the plant. Several hectares of secluded property. With a bridge too, over the creek."

"The creek the town is named after?" Raul asks.

"Yes, that creek." She looks around and lowers her voice. "They're hostile to townspeople who go bear their land. I don't think they'd be any nicer to an outsider."

This waitress is telling him a lot for someone who'd just breezed into town, Raul thought, as she lingered over his table. What does she want from him?

"I wanted to see that creek, you know. That's why I'm staying."

"Where are you staying?" she asks.

"A motel. I hear there's one a couple of roads away."

"Mr. Mike's. His is the only place around here, but it's an okay place."

She lingers some more, and Raul looks up and thanks her in a tone that gives her the impression that he is done talking. He eats his food ravenously and puts a couple of bills on the table for her, with a generous tip. She is the only person in this town whom he'd met that had volunteered information. Not his way or the army's, whose rule was strictly no volunteering. He gets up and walks out. The three couples are still at their tables, sipping their coffee and doing whatever else they are doing. He catches the waitress's eye and nods to her.

The sun is not as hot when he gets outside, and he goes straight in the direction of the motel. He gets in, finds the owner agreeable, pays for two nights, and gets his keys. It isn't much of a hotel, but he's slept in worse, and this is as comfortable as he'll get in a while. He takes a long shower and when he comes out and changes clothes, he decides to take a walk. He knows exactly where he is going. The keys are dropped off at the reception as he takes off. The time on the clock is around 5 PM. He knows the workers will start heading home now and their cars will be all over the streets on the way home, but he keeps going. He passes the diner and sees the same waitress in it. He waves at her, but he doesn't think she sees him. Then he sees the stream of cars coming from far off ahead. The plant is that way, and the creek, the other.

He leaves Main Street and begins walking through backways to prevent being seen and raising suspicions. From the cop and the waitresses' attitude, they are scared of the Duncans. He doesn't care because all he wants to see is the creek. But he also doesn't want to be seen until he finds out more about the Duncans. There's no use getting himself tangled up with them before he knows anything of value.

He keeps walking, and before long, he can no longer hear the sounds of vehicles getting back from work. The road ahead gets quieter and no vehicle even moves, He walks some more, and he hears the rumble of an engine. He hides behind shrubbery and sees a truck cross a little bridge several feet from him and turns the other way, away from the town. He stays where he is for about an hour, just to see what will happen, and sure enough, another truck drives in from the same direction. It soon leaves.

He can't keep hiding behind the shrubbery before it gets too dark to see the creek, so he comes out and keeps walking in the direction of the bridge.

A Jeep comes out of the bridge and he can't hide quickly enough before the driver sees him, so he just keeps walking. The Jeep stops and a young man hops out. He looks like a failed football jock, and he sounds like one.

"What are you doing out here, old man? I've never seen you before, but you should know better than to wander, shouldn't you?"

Raul gazes at him evenly and moves past him.

"I didn't say you could leave, bastard. I'm talking to you. You're on my land and you're in my power. Get it,"

Raul smiles and replies,

"The only people's power I've ever been under are my parents and Uncle Sam. You don't count, you spit-wad, so get out of my way."

The boy's eyes narrow, and he lunges at Raul without thinking. Overconfident in his size. But Raul knows that his bulk makes him slow and that most of it are steroids, none of it built from training and real-life combat experience.

Raul doesn't move until the guy has nearly made contact. Then he sidesteps him and lands a solid hit in the side of his ribs. He hears a satisfying crunch, and the guy goes down. Raul never wastes any time with opponents, and he goes in to make sure that this one is down for the count. He kicks him twice in the belly and on his head to make sure he is out. He then drags the guy into the Jeep, starts it, and parks it out of view of the road. He gets out and goes to see his creek. It is muddy, water flowering in crooked lines. The Duncans, he is sure, and their suspicions shipments. He decides that daylight is too bright to see the rest of the Duncan land, so he quits and goes back to the diner.

It is more occupied than it was at noon, with most age-grades getting representation, but it is not full. The waitresses from earlier are still here so he goes directly to her.

"What the hell is going on with the Duncans and this town?" He demands in a not-so-low voice.

A couple of patrons turn to look at him and immediately go back to their drinks.

"Not so loud, mister. The people don't like to hear that name even though it keeps food on their table."

He sits at the countertop where customers can sit to just get coffee and look at her.

"I'm listening."

"And I'm working. But I'll talk."

"The Duncans have been in Pryor Creek for some generations now, and their wealth got started by bootlegging during the prohibition. These days, nobody knows what they do, apart from the plant, but they still are very wealthy, no doubt of that." She pauses to wipe a stain.

"But that's not the issue. What is, is that the town is terrified of them. Once in a while, they show up in town and exert their power, because, in reality, they own this town. Everybody is in their pocket and we can't complain or we'll be kicked out. My parents took a loan from them to buy this diner and were soon in debt. They own it now but allow me to work it. If I move against them in any way, it'll be taken from me, just like that." She leaves with a customer's order and comes back.

"And that's not even all." She looks around, even more, cautious this time, and her voice goes lower. "There are rumors."

"What kind?" he inquires,

"Kids have been going missing, people that owed debts too, gone, just like that. No one can question them to even verify these things."

"What about the police?"

"Forget about them, mister. I said the Duncans own everybody. There's nothing we can do."

Raul muses and asks if anybody has been on their land before.

"Not anyone that has come out to tell us. The entire clan is out there, so I don't think it is even possible."

Raul nods and stands to go.

"What are you going to do?" she asks, a pleading look in her eye.

"Go find answers," he replies and leaves the diner. The bell tinkles in his absence.

×××

He goes back to the motel to rest a little before it gets dark, wondering why nobody has come for him yet. Has nobody found the guy he beat up?

Night comes, and he begins his trek again. As he comes to the shrubbery where he hid earlier in the day, he notices that the Jeep is no longer where he parked it. *How long ago was it discovered, and what action will follow,* he wonders.

He doesn't have to wonder for long when three vehicles drive out of the entrance to the property in the direction of town. He is sure they are going to look for him, to meet their justice as they see fit.

He stays out for five minutes and makes sure no other vehicles are coming out, then he moves, He runs at a light speed over the bridge and crosses the fence at a side of the woods far from the gate.

Once inside, he can see several structures. All houses, probably belonging to each family member. There is what looks like a big barn up in the distance, and only the light in one house is turned on. That means one family member didn't go out to join in the hunt. That leaves them and the security at the gate. A total of what he estimates to be four people. He moves around the property, checking out things for himself, and he doesn't find anything of interest until he gets to the barn. He picks the lock and gets in and sees that the interior is not a barn. It is a warehouse for cocaine, and that explains the trucks that kept coming and going at noon. He goes deeper into the barn and finds a locked door. He picks it too, and what he discovers in it hits him hard.

Polaroids upon Polaroids of kids and adults being tortured and abused hung on one side of the wall, and recording equipment stans closed, but on the ready, pointed at the other side of the wall. The room smells metallic, and he is enraged.

He goes out of the barn towards what he's ascertained is the garage and picks up a gallon of gasoline and a lighter. He sprinkles it all over the barn, and then he goes outside and lights the lighter, pauses a bit to catch his breath, and flings it in. It goes up in flames almost immediately.

Sure enough, screams come from the house and the gate, and the occupants run to the barn, but he is no longer there. He has found the keys to one Jeep in the garage, and he has steered it to point in the direction of the barn. Four people are clustered outside the fire, shouting, and doing nothing. He guns the Jeep and is on them before they can do anything. The sound of bones crunched is not as loud as the fire licking up all that timber, crackling. He reverses, puts the car in gear, and goes again. He crushes the bones properly and drives over the four of them. He drives towards the gate, sure that the fire is spreading, and is high enough to be seen from town.

He parks the Jeep at one of the pillars and pulls out one of the remaining two gallons of gasoline in the car. He pours it all over the car and the gatehouse. He then puts a short string in the other can, and stands by, waiting for the angry sound of engines to reach him.

Soon enough, it does, and he lights the string. As the Duncans are driving into their property, the flame touches the gasoline and it blows up. The three cars go flying, and in mid-air, their tanks explode, too. It rains fire, and Raul takes off running.

×××

The next morning at the diner, he smiles at the waitress.

"Such a lovely town you've got here. It's a shame I'll have to leave today."

"Thank you for taking care of our problem, Mister," she says, meaning every word.

"What problem?" he asks as a sly smile spreads over his face.

She smiles back, and when he goes outside the diner, the cop is waiting outside for him to drop him off where he picks him.

"One day, huh?" he says in the way of conversation. He doesn't get a reply.

When he gets dropped off, the cop whisper "Thank you," to him before driving off.

Raul sticks his thumb out for a ride.

VINCE

"...Fuck."

Henry slammers the little glass cup on the table. That is the third time he is doing it tonight. The bartender gives him a face and contemplates in his mind whether or not to give this particular gentleman any more shots. Everyone, who had previously sat around Henry had drawn further and further away from him. Now it is just him, sitting significantly alone by the bartender's table. Henry doesn't seem to care one bit about what is happening around him, though. He is thoroughly agitated.

"Hey." Henry points at the bartender with his index finger; his remaining four fingers still holding the cup; "Another."

The bartender hesitates, Henry notices,

"I said, another," he retorts, His voice slightly higher this time.

"Whoa, whoa. Take it easy."

A middle-aged man wearing a leather jacket approaches him. Henry doesn't seem impressed.

"I'm gonna have you take it easy right there, buddy."

"The fuck are you going to do if I don't?"

"Well, if you're going to keep drinking like that, then I'm afraid I can't allow you to drive home tonight. You might be a danger to yourself..." The man says, and then flashes the inner side of his jacket to reveal a police badge. He is a cop.

"...and to others."

Henry rolls his eyes.

"Tch."

He turns back to the bartender and pushes the cup toward him.

"Another."

He then turns to face the cop.

"It's not my first time drinking. I've not even had up to half of what it takes for me to lose it. Besides..."

Henry brings out a badge of his own, slightly different from the officer's; and shows it to the cop.

"We're in the same line of business."

"Ah. Detective Henry, it says."

"Indeed."

"I've seen you around the province. You're currently working on a case, aren't you? Is that what's making you take multiple shots in tandem? You hit a snag?"

"Snag," Henry gulped down another shot in one go and exhaled; "is an understatement. It undermines the severity of the situation. It's like; I'm currently at a point, where I can't even do anything anymore, and I have to wait for the culprit to make his next move."

The officer sits down next to him. He seems interested.

"...oof. Sounds like a very bad place for any official to be...; especially a detective."

The officer signals to the bartender to pour Henry another shot.

"Wanna talk about it?"

Henry pauses, Ideally, it isn't exactly ethical to reveal the details of a case that is still open to anyone; even if the person is a fellow officer of the law, like himself. But he feels like he has hit rock bottom. Deep down, he couldn't care less about the confidentiality of the case anymore. He doesn't think that telling the officer about it will affect the situation in any way at all and besides, he also doesn't mind telling someone who might actually be able to understand his frustrations about it, because talking to his wife or friends about it, was always a complete waste of time.

"Seven years. Seven. Years. For seven years I've tried to solve this particular case. It's happened three times over the past seven years. The first time it happened, I couldn't solve it, and because it didn't happen for a while after that, I had practically dismissed it, hoping it wouldn't happen again. The second time it happened, I thought I could smell traits that were very similar to the first occurrence. Now it's happening a third time. There's no doubt about it. All three cases seem different but are all definitely linked. It's the same person. The same murderer."

The officer takes a shot of his own.

"What makes this particular murderer so difficult to catch that you've been unable to get him after seven years? Especially now that you've linked him to his previous attacks?"

"The bastard doesn't kill people the conventional way. Each time he embarks on one of his 'streaks', he uses a different method from the previous streak. It's why I was unable to link the first two murdering streaks to each other in the first place. They seem different. But they aren't. It's the same guy, different methods. I know it."

"How can you tell?"

"Because there's another link between the murders. There are three links between each of the murdering streaks. The first is the method used. All who die during a particular streak, die of the same cause. It's how you can tell it's from the same source. The second is the number of people that die; five, each time. All five of them, dying from the same thing."

"Of course. The murderer gives himself away like that." The officer paused, and then took another shot; "But what's the third link between the murders?"

Henry's eyes narrow.

"The reason for the murders."

Henry gulps down another shot and then slams the glass cup so hard against the table that it breaks right from the base. Everyone in the bar then falls into a sudden hush. They all turn to look at Henry, who pays no attention to them and continues to stare at the broken cup with contempt. Almost as though he is mad at it for breaking.

The bartender has had enough. He gives Henry a warning face, as though trying to tell him that he only has one last straw to break. Henry doesn't look at the bartender. He simply pushes the broken glass shards aside with the back of his arm and then buries his head in his arms.

"Hey... you good?"

"It's a sick fucker. A fucking psychopath. It doesn't even make any sense. I mean, it makes sense; but it's a completely ridiculous reason to kill people. I'm no psychologist, but that kind of thinking probably developed at a young age. And now, it's every and anyone around him that could suffer for it. It's unsettling; the thought that you could be the next one to die, based simply on the first letter of your name."

"Name...?" The officer sat up, and leaned toward Henry; "What do the names have to do with it?"

"The killer chooses his victims by the first letter of their names. Random people, completely unrelated in any aspect. It all depends on the first letter of their first names. It happened in the first streak, the second, and now even in this one. It's why it's almost impossible to tell who the murderer would strike next because there could literally be thousands of options."

"You're still keeping me in a fine amount of suspense. What do the names have to do with the deaths?"

"Victoria Andersen. Igor Stravinsky. Nami Tokoyama. Catherine Rogue. All of them; four different, apparently random deaths over the past two months. Linked only by the cause of death; a chemical, that kills them slowly over time and the first letters of their names."

Henry raises his head to look at the officer. His face is distraught.

"You see, the killer has a kink. He gets off of killing people in the particular order of spelling his first name. His name is Vince. That's all we know about him. Vince. But over five thousand people are bearing that name in this locality alone. It's not enough to find him. And so he keeps killing people, spelling his name. It was the same for his first streak, his second, and now this. The V, in Victoria. The I in Igor. The N, the C. It's his stupid little game. Spelling his name using his victims. His next victim's name will start with an E. That's all I know about it. There are also thousands of people whose first names start with an E. I can't possibly hope to protect all of them. He doesn't even kill them conventionally. He kills them slowly; poisoning them with a highly undetectable chemical that they'll ingest over time until it accumulates in their bodies and kills them. It almost doesn't look like a murder at all. But it's targeted, and so it's detectable. An autopsy always gives him away. It's how I've linked the murders up to this point. But..."

Henry sinks back into his arms.

"It's not enough. Even if I know where and how he's going to strike next. There's nothing I can do to stop him until the victim is already dead. The truth only comes out when it's too late. The chemical isn't hard to get or make. It's used generally. Grown in gardens. It's everywhere. The names aren't enough either. Too many possible targets. It's driving me crazy. At this rate, I might never be able to catch the culprit. He's just going to keep killing and killing, and killing people, making their deaths spell his fucking name, until—"

Henry is interrupted by a phone call. He pulls his phone out of his pocket to look at who it is. On seeing the caller, the look on his face is relaxed. It is probably someone he cares about. He picked it up and suddenly speaks very calmly.

"Hey, I—"

The person on the other side of the call is speaking frantically.

"What?"

The frantic rant continues,

"What do you mean? Where's Emily?"

The caller speaks for a little while longer. Henry's facial expression starts to change. It regresses, from worry to shock and then into fear.

"Oh my God."

He cuts the call and suddenly makes for the door. He trips and falls over almost immediately, as though he lost his strength.

"Whoa." The officer rushes to help him up; "Are you okay?"

"I have to go. It's my daughter; it's Emily. I have to get to her."

"Oh. Shit." The officer pulled him up swiftly and helped him toward the door; "If something's happened to your daughter, then you do have to get to her immediately. Let's find out where you're parked."

The officer helps Henry to the door, and then to his car. Henry, on the other hand, finds his strength leaving his body, as he slowly progresses towards his car. He feels like he is losing control and motor function of his limbs; his hands, his legs, his mouth, and then ultimately, everything. By the time Henry gets to his car, he is completely unable to move.

"Phew," the officer sighs, as he plops Henry unto the driver's seat; "You're heavier than you look."

Henry can say and do nothing, except stare at the officer, with confusion, and a desire for help etches into his eyes.

"It's aconite. The damn bartender didn't know it was in the bottle. I know you like to drink whiskey, so I snuck a little aconite in there. I tweaked the dose, though so it'll only make you immobile for a little while. You should be moving again in a few hours. I guess that's more than enough time for me."

Henry can't even widen his eyes, as the realization of what is happening starts to set in.

"Mahn. You pay attention to detail, detective Henry. I have to give credit, where credit is due. You actually got everything right. The link between the murders. The victims. The reason for the murders. The name streak; everything. I mean; you figured everything out. And this is only my third strike!"

Henry wants to say something, but can't.

"I feel like... You would definitely eventually have caught me if I decided to do another streak after this. Somehow, you'd just figure it out, and then I'd get had. It's crazy. This has been an eye-opener for me. I'll have to move more carefully next time."

The officer leans in to look directly into Henry's eyes.

"Our little game is complete. The last letter is E. E, to complete the puzzle; the puzzle is VINCE. Me. E, as luck would have it, for Emily, as well the name of your beautiful, beautiful daughter. I'm sure the call you received earlier told you all about how she was unable to move and is dying and you should get there fast and all of that. There's nothing you can do about it, though. It's going to kill her. She's probably already dead by now. My name is complete. You lost this round as well."

The officer tucks Henry into the seat and shuts the door.

"I'm leaving, Henry. I'm going away. Far away. somewhere completely outside your jurisdiction, and your reach. I'm afraid you and I won't be meeting, ever again. I'm sorry about your daughter, you know. She was such a sweet girl. I wouldn't have had to do this to her if you weren't CUTTING TOO CLOSE, INTO MY BUSINESS!"

The officer raises his voice and then exhales and brushes his hair back. He returns to his normal tone.

"But it is what it is. The game's over now. I've won. I'll have to find someone else to play with. It's crazy, really. Every time a detective thinks he's almost won, I still always come out on top. I really am, always one step ahead."

He turns to look at Henry and smiles,

"You're still young, Henry. I'm sure you can make another daughter. But don't come looking for me."

He starts walking away, waving to Henry as he leaves.

"Or I'll make sure you lose that one, too."

STALKER

The worst part about being in a dark place is all the waiting. Perhaps, you need to remain at that spot for a while until it is safe enough to leave. The second worst part is that the most unexpected things happen when you are in the dark.

The darkness makes adrenaline spike. I imagine lighting a cigarette and inhaling it, trying to resist the temptation to stand, and taking to my heels. I feel nervous. There is a reason for that. Nora had been my best friend and we shared an apartment. There is nothing to worry about. She is a cop. I bet that she can protect herself out there. Despite that, I have a sneaking suspicion that something bad might have happened to Nora.

I hide in a compartment in my closet, clutching the locket I wear around my neck; my heart is pounding. I close the sliding door and crouch so that no one can see me.

Paint flakes off the door and I pick at it with my shuddering fingers. Someone has used the same method to scratch two sets of initials next to where I am crouching, then surrounded it with the drawing of a withered maple leaf and added the date. I close my eyes. Will I ever get used to the shock of seeing the evidence of the last time an intruder had broken into my bedroom without my knowledge? The lemon scent wafts through the air.

A couple of minutes. Then four. The door squeaks open and then footsteps advance towards me.

xxx

I clutch the hem of my white nightgown. My palms become clammy, feeling rooted to the spot.

A hand makes its way into the closet, and I push myself to the back so that I can remain unnoticed. I hold down my breath, gulping down my breath to stay quiet. Unexpectedly, the hand grabs me and pulls me out.

A shadow falls across my face and I open my eyes. A man is standing over me. He is wearing a black t-shirt and a pair of white shorts. My nose wrinkles at a familiar scent and I quickly realize that it was my boyfriend, Duke.

I didn't expect that Duke would show up at that time but his presence brought me some relief. "Sorry, I thought it was someone else," I say as I sweep my hands across my forehead to get rid of sweat.

Duke holds my hand and leads me to my bed. He helps me to sit and then sits beside me. For the briefest moments, I feel as if the dread and darkness that sat across the center of my soul has been lit with a light lighter than the sun. The weight that had pressed down on me lifted and vanished.

A second later, Duke wraps his arms around my shoulder and pulls me in to hug. My arms squeeze me a bit tighter, and I breathe more slowly; my warmth melting into his as every component in my body loses its tension to the quietness of the bedroom. His warm hug is soothing to me.

×××

For a long time, Duke silently glances at me as if he can hear my thoughts. I feel so happy that he is sitting right beside me on my bed, watching over me. Duke is always there when I need him; my favorite shoulder to lean on.

At that moment, I am worried about my friend. A phrase keeps repeating in my head. It's past 11 pm and Nora has not arrived from work. But I brush it off. I assure myself that she will be okay.

"Why did you hide in your closet? I looked for you." Duke asks.

I weigh up how much I should tell Duke. I dare not tell him the entire details because I know that he will worry too much about it. Whatever the case, I can handle that issue alone. I don't want to get Duke worked up.

"I feel like someone is stalking me."

Duke's eyes fall open. "Why didn't you tell me before this time?"

"I don't want to bother you over small things. Plus, Nora is a cop. She can work around it," I admit,

Duke nods, putting his hand on mine. "But you should have told me. You could have died. Nora can't raise the dead," he says in a matter-of-fact tone.

I feel a twinge of regret, an urge to apologize for trying to hide my problems from Duke. But I end up apologizing. I love him that much. I am pretty sure that he wouldn't trade any woman for me, too.

"I won't keep you in the dark anymore. You know how much I love you, right?"

Duke looks at me steadily, cupping my face with his hands. "I forgive you but on one condition." He smiles,

I am curious about Duke's condition. But it is obvious. He can't ask me to move out of my house and stay with him at his lone apartment. Duke has brought up that suggestion umpteen times, but I told him no. This day won't be different. I want to complete my master's degree in fashion design before I will take any huge step. In all honesty, I am just scared.

We have been dating for almost two years now. I met Duke during my final year at the undergraduate school when he was in graduate school. He and Nora were childhood friends. After she moved into my dorm and we became friends, she insisted that I met him. Nora said that we'd make a good couple and she was right. We made it official only after a date and since then, things had been wonderful.

The thought of moving in with Duke seems so final as if I will be closing a chapter. I know that once I take that step, the next step is marriage and I am not ready for that. I haven't told Duke yet, but aside from earning a master's degree, I want to set up a big fashion designing shop before marriage. I haven't had the chance to design outside the box since I started working in a second-tier fashion designing firm. I will turn twenty-three in a couple of weeks, so age is still on my side.

Duke snaps me out of my thoughts. "Earth to Ella!" he says, brushing my hair away from my neck with his hand. " Do you mind listening to my condition?"

I stare at Duke and he is watching me. Then a slow grin appears across his face. The way he's looking at me is causing my heart to race, so I regain my composure with a few words. "You were going to ask me to move in with you anyway. I've nothing to hear," I snap,

Duke nodded, laughing. "I was not going to ask you that." He closes the space between us and presses his lips to my neck and kisses his way down my collarbone. "I was going to ask you to kiss me. After the kiss, we would decide how to get rid of that stalker."

"You, kiss thief," I tease, smiling at Duke.

Duke looks amused, silently taking me in. "Kiss me," he says. I do,

We start kissing like crazy as if our lives depend on it.

I begin to picture the stalker. I always see the shadow of a lady wearing a ripped pair of jeans and a mask that conceals her face. When I am walking and only when I am in my house, I turn around and before I know it, she has disappeared. She is always seven steps away from me. The stalker never makes a noise but just a pregnant silence.

The stalker emanates a feeling of dread as if she has polluted the air around her. She always makes the atmosphere feel dark and gloomy in a second and that is how I know that she is around. The stalker often turns her back to me, so I have never seen her face. I wonder how she looks like and I wonder what she wants from me. The last time I checked, I didn't have a grudge against anyone. I am an easy-going person.

We kiss again.

"I want more, Duke. Give me more."

The sound of Duke's cell phone ringing in his pocket reaches my ears. It takes the force of my will to break apart from him. He rolls out of bed and stands.

"Forgive me. I need to pick the call at the verandah," Duke sighs, tugging out his phone from his pocket.

I nod. "No worries. I'll be waiting here," I snap, watching him cross to the verandah.

It's already an hour and Duke hasn't returned from the verandah. For some strange reason, I want to make my way out of my bedroom to find him. The realization makes me more anxious. That young man has never bothered me. I hope he won't do so this day.

With determined strides, I breeze out of my room, crossing to the parlor. In a matter of minutes, I reach the verandah. Once I get there, a sudden coldness hits my core. I drop to my knees from a perceived fright and it feels like I might pass out in a second.

×××

Once that first tear breaks free, the rest follow in an unbroken stream. My face soaks in my tears as I duck behind Duke's corpse on the ground. The sickening odor of blood and dirt hang around the verandah like stinky smoke. Duke's mouth is covered with a black mask; a counterpoint to the rest of his face. Fresh blood pools around his body. Two maple leaves scrawled in blood are stuck around his throat.

The horrible sight makes my brain falter for a moment. I have a hunch that the stalker must be the brain behind Duke's death. The maple leaves on his body must have some sort of connection with her. Suddenly, I start questioning the fact that I allowed him to pick a call at the verandah. I should have suggested a safer option.

"What in the world had I done to deserve this?" I screamed. "Why did this have to happen?"

On their own accord, my fingers trace the contours of the locket I am wearing. Within the second opening, is a picture of us—Duke and I. We'd taken that picture on our last date night. It was, to date, one of my happiest memories. My eyes glaze with more tears as I look at the picture, then at Duke's body.

"I should have moved into your house and spent more time with you when I could." My voice breaks and I cry some more. "I can't even do that now."

As soon as I manage to reach out and run a finger down Duke's cheek, I feel a hostile brush on my shoulder. In a couple of seconds, I feel a repeated hit on the back of my head and I pass out. That is simply the only thing I can recall.

It feels as though the world has closed in on me.

×××

Two weeks later.

It hurts. Everything hurts—the light in my eyes and the pain in my head. My nose is bleeding and I wipe it with my hands.

"Ella?"

The voice emerges through a fog of pain. I try to nod but words can't come out of my mouth. Her voice hurts.

"Ella, you are safe. You are at a hospital. You will have a scan soon."

It's a woman wearing a black leather dress and a pair of heels. She helps me to sit up on the hospital bed and sits beside me. Who is she?

"Is there anyone we should call?"

I shake my head.

"Don't move your head," she says, "you have a concussion."

"Nora," I whisper,

"You want me to call Nora?" The woman sighs. "You are asking me to call the wrong person. She confessed to stalking you and killing your boyfriend because she believed that you snatched him from her. She told my colleagues and me two days ago at our custody."

My eyes widen, "What?"

"Your boyfriend's mother wants to press murder charges against her. She won't go scot-free. Just try to relax."

THE ARRANGEMENT

It's another chill November morning. A cold breeze caresses my skin and treats me like the queen I deserve to be. It trails every inch from my hair to my feet and assures me of a promising Friday filled with bliss. *What a way to start my day,* I think. I turn my face to the other side of the bed, smiling with eyes closed, savoring the rich feel of my silver linen sheets, only for the sun to announce its presence -my cue. I want to open my eyes and confirm that I'm not late, that the sun hasn't risen, and I can savor this moment some minutes more. But my subconscious knows it's all a farce I'm making up in my head to please my lazy ass.

I open my eyes and the first thing they land on is my alarm clock that is flashing 8:30 AM at my smooched-up face.

"Crap!" I say and jolt out of bed like a deer.

I brush and bathe in what felt like two milliseconds then dive into my thigh-high black leather shorts with a cotton pink top. With a jacket in hand and my book bag in another, I head downstairs like a speedster with extra pair of legs.

Today would be the worst day to get to school late; the very worst. I'd never win the elections if I did. Weeks of hard work would go down the drain and my team wouldn't let me hear the last of it. Plus, they believe in me too much for me to let them down.

"Hey, Missy," Uncle Leon calls from behind the kitchen counter where he is preparing breakfast. "Where are you running to. Don't you want to have breakfast?"

I so want to decline and dash to school but I don't want to send him wrong signals. Since I lost both my parents to the car accident, he's been the only family member that cared.

"Sure, I will, Uncle Leon," I say with the warmest smile on my face.

Other factors aside, he looks too damn happy for me to decline. I join him to set the table to make things a bit faster and we sit together to eat. Spicy Korean Pork Sandwich and red wine? If I didn't have amnesia or something I'd think it's my birthday.

"What a luxurious breakfast, Uncle Leon, what's the occasion? I mean, Pinot Noir in the morning?" I ask while downing the glass of wine.

"Oh, nothing," he says, trying so hard but failing woefully at concealing a very stubborn but beautiful smile that forced its way on his face.

"Oh, is someone in love?" I ask the first crazy question that comes to my mind.

Uncle Leon and I live alone but I've caught him a couple of times whispering and giggling over the phone at odd hours, and no one can tell me he's been doing that with a 'friend', that'd be absurd. Especially for him.

"What? Shut up," he says in between chuckles and gets up to take his plate back to the kitchen.

Uncle Leon isn't as built and buff as many girls would like their boyfriends to be, but he has the personality of a guardian angel. He's a great companion, patient listener, and he knows just what to say to a weary heart and when to say it. He is pretty good with conversations too- probably where I got that trait from. My parents were freaking introverts but I'm quite the opposite. There is no dull moment with him. His only problem is his anger issue. Whenever he gets angry, the whole earth must tremble; it's always so ugly. But in all, Uncle Leon is a great guy. I mean, I won't have a roof over my head if he isn't.

"See you soon," I say and kiss him on his cheek before leaving. "And don't forget your class with us by noon," I yell over my shoulders.

"I won't," he says and slurps in his wine, and I find my way down to the university.

The once sunny sky was already paving way for gray clouds. It's the early times in November; two hours of sunlight is something to be grateful for. I alight from the bus and head over to the university premises to catch up with my friends.

The election is to hold in the main auditorium which is a bit far from the entrance. On top of that, I have to struggle my way through the crowd of students that flocked the hallways and corridors. The university is a very busy place and on a normal day, filled with hundreds of millions of students from far and wide.

"Hey!" Emma yells when she catches sight of me in the crowd.

She stands beside one of the tall pillars of the school building, waving her hand in the air for me to notice and find my way to her.

"You're late!" she says.

"I know, I know. I'm here now. Chill out," I say and give her the brightest smile of the century but trust Emma not to be moved by it, not even a single bit.

We walk into the auditorium filled with students. A panel of the university's electoral committee sitting on stage, behind the podium.

"Emma!" Matteo calls a few rows ahead of us where he had reserved seats.

We exchange pleasantries and take our seats. I sit right next to Matteo - in between him and Emma - and I roll my eyes when I notice him fiddling with his fingers and tapping his feet. It's too easy to tell when he is nervous. I was his girlfriend for two years, I would know. He must be uncomfortable with the fact of having me sitting too close to him because his new girlfriend is close by. Well, that's his problem. I've also got mine- asides from the election. There are several things that I want to fall in place today.

"They're about to announce, fingers crossed," Emma says.

"And the University's new President of the Student Administration is..." the chairman says from the front of the hall.

"Babe, come on, cross fingers with us," Emma says to Matteo.

"Nah, baby, I'm good."

"Don't be such a downer, come on," I say. He smiles and crosses fingers with us.

The next thing I know, the whole crowd is cheering. The screams are so loud, I feel like my eardrums are going to burst anytime soon. I look up only to see my picture displayed on the screen with Student Administration President 2021 under my name. I stand frozen for a few seconds. I can't believe it. I mean my friends and I put a lot of work into my campaign and all that, but I won. Emma shakes me ruggedly, madly glad I won, and so I am. I walk up on stage to receive my plaque and take pictures with the committee. The crowd cheers even louder. Not to brag but I'm quite popular and loved by a lot of students in the university and I knew I had a high chance at winning this election, especially with my friends by my side. But at the same time, I couldn't have been so sure. But I won anyway and I'm freaking glad I did.

My friends and I leave the auditorium to go celebrate. On our way out, we see my uncle. He approaches us with a stiff glare, staring straight at Matteo and I roll my eyes again knowing what that face means. Before he gets to us, Emma excuses herself and leaves for the restroom.

"Professor Leon, how are you today?" Matteo says with a shaky laugh and my uncle doesn't even budge; I think his face even turned sterner. "Save it, Matt," he says, Matteo swallows.

"Uncle Leo...," I say. My uncle clears his throat and stops me.

"I mean, Professor Miller."

"Yes?" he says.

"You don't really have to be stern with Matt all the time. I already told you we made up," I say.

"Made up! After what he did to you?"

"Exactly. To me. And I'm over it. Can you get over it too?" I say and he walks away but not before giving Matteo a death stare.

I guess he is tired of my uncle's threats. I'm also tired because I've tried several times to take it off his mind, but nothing has worked. I just hope it doesn't get beyond vocal threats; I know what my uncle can do when he's angry. He is nothing better than a mutated beast in that state.

"I'm going to check on Emma," Matteo says.

"Yeah, you should. She's taking too long,"

He runs along to find Emma and me sitting by one of the windows of the building waiting for them. A couple of people pass and congratulated me for winning the election. A few of them I know, and we have minor conversations but after a long time, I grow tired and leave to search for Matteo and Emma.

I check the bathroom on the ground floor -that was the floor we were on when she left- but she wasn't there, and

128

Matteo wasn't either. I go up to the next floor, then the next, and the one after that. Still no sign of the two love birds. *Did they think they could elope and leave me here, those two?* I've checked every bathroom in the admin building except for the one on the first floor. So, I head over there ASAP and I find Matteo.

"Hey, have you seen Emma?" he asks.

"No, you haven't found her?" I ask.

"Apparently not. I've searched every bathroom in this building. I even tried calling."

"And?" I ask.

"No luck with that either. She's not picking up."

"That's strange," I say. "Emma is always with her cellphone twenty-four seven."

"Exactly," Matteo says. "Should we call the cops?"

"It's not been twenty-four hours yet; I doubt they'll want to attend to us."

"But she's missing! And it's no joke, I can't fucking find her!" he says.

"Calm down, Matt. Freaking out won't help. We have to stay calm to think, okay?" I say. Then I leave him to alert security and the whole university.

Emma has been missing for hours and nobody knows where she is. I walk down the halls and I see worry and fear on the faces of other students that have heard the news. This is not the first case of a missing student; two others have disappeared like this before. And what is that they say about the third time? God knows if I don't find Emma, that would be one less wish that will be granted today. I've won the election, but Emma is more important to me right now.

I run down to the ground floor again and I spot my uncle in his car a few feet away from the admin block. I walk towards him and stop in my tracks when I get close enough to the car. We both stared at each other for a few seconds.

"Get in," my uncle says.

I turn to the passenger's door and hop into the car. The ride back home is awfully quiet. What's happening in school is no child's play and it keeps our mind occupied with several thoughts; nothing must go wrong with Emma; nothing at all.

Thirty minutes into the ride, my uncle takes a turn that I don't know. The street looks familiar like I've been here before, but I don't quite remember much. He stops in front of a yellow duplex and turns the car engine off. I could only tell whose house it is when I see Matteo's elder brother leave the apartment a few seconds after we arrive.

"In the kitchen," my uncle says and brings out a key and hands it to me.

"Thank you. For everything," I say and smile lightly.

I head to the front of the house and open the front door with the key my uncle gave me. I search the entire place till I finally found something odd in the kitchen downstairs. It's a huge black plastic bag on the floor, one of those they put the bodies in. It keeps shaking like something is moving inside. Or someone moving inside. I walk over to the bag and unzip it asap.

"Oh, Emma," I say when I finally set eyes on her inside the bag.

She gasps for air as I open it. Her hands and feet are bound in cable ties and her mouth is gagged with gaffa tape. There are tears all over her face; the poor thing must have been crying for a long time. I lift her into one of the chairs in the kitchen and take the tape off her mouth.

"I'm so glad you're here, please get me out of this place," she cries. I look deep into her teary eyes. Seeing her this way is really something. If Matteo comes back and sees her like this, his heart will be shattered into tiny miserable pieces -the goal."

"I can't, Emma," I say, still looking into her eyes.

She freezes and looks at me, too.

"What?" she says.

"If I let you go, how else will I make Matteo pay for raping me. He took my virginity without my consent because of his recklessness and selfishness, Emma," I say, and tears start to trickle down my cheeks.

"But you said you were over that. You said you moved on!"

"Yes. I said, Emma. I didn't mean it," I say and draw out a pocketknife from my jacket.

"No, no, you can't do this. We're friends! We're fucking friends!" she starts to yell.

"I'm really sorry, Emma," I say and slit her throat wide open without second thoughts.

I stand and watch her blood flow down her neck down to her clothes and into the bag she was still in. I lean forward to check her pulse but my watch beeps as my uncle said it would and I make for the backyard which is just outside the kitchen.

"Angelo," Matteo calls when he enters the house. "Why on earth did you leave the door open?"

He locks the door and walks into the living room. On his way up the stairs, I see him turn towards the kitchen. Smart-ass quickly caught a glimpse of something odd. He walks in only to find his girlfriend covered in a pool of blood.

"Emma!" he screamed and held his hair tight like he was going to pull them off.

He runs to pick her up and keeps yelling her name as the dead could hear. LOL. I watch for a few seconds as he suffers, and I smile.

ALL WAS A LIE

It's around 3 am and the roads are dead silent outside the hotel 'My Way'. But the inside of the hotel is booming with the sound of music and the crowd is hooting and dancing all around the dance floor. In the crowd, someone just popped another bottle of champagne, and a new wave of cheers has begun. The whole crowd is enjoying the New Year night, oblivious to the fact that the fate of their country for the next five years is being written beneath them.

In the basement, there is a big wide lounge which is secluded from the rest of the hotel. The room is guarded against all sides and the guests are entering from the underground door.

A man in his late sixties enters the room and instantly, the slight conversation inside the hall goes silent. The man opens the button of his suit and sits at the crown seat in the lounge which had been left empty for him.

"I am pleased by your decision." The man starts a conversation, directing at the person sitting right next to him.

"It's all thanks to you, sir," another man replies, who looks like in his mid-fifties.

"Congratulations to all of you, Mr. Anderson has been selected to serve us all. The ball is in our court now," the old man addresses all the people in the hall.

All people start clapping for Mr. Anderson, who stands with pride and bends slightly to thank everyone.

"Mr. Anderson, meet your new cabinet. They will guide you all the way to your success. Welcome to our party," the old man announces again cheerfully, and the members start clapping again.

Soon, a couple of waiters enter and start serving glasses of champagne and along with a complimentary gift from the host, Mr. Anderson, which everyone accepts wholeheartedly because they know the price of the selection awaits inside the gifts.

It's the best night for Mr. Anderson. Everything is going according to his plan. Now the only wait is for tomorrow's sun to rise and shed light on his new bright future.

×××

'Artemis Heights' a twenty-two floored residential building stood tall and proud waiting for the sun to indi-

135

cate the new beginnings but unfortunately, the sun is nowhere close to come. In the morning around eight, dark black clouds start gathering in the sky. People are running to their work with the excitement of the New Year.

The same hustle-bustle can be seen in the main street in front of Artemis Heights. A woman running with a wide smile and an umbrella in her hand runs across the footpath and hails a taxi. The taxi stops at the side of the service line. She settles inside and closes the door.

The taxi is about to roll down when suddenly, out of nowhere, with a loud crash, a man falls right on the windscreen of the taxi. The siren of the car goes on and gradually, people start gathering around them. The girl with the umbrella gets out of the car crying and shouting but no one is currently listening to her. People are gawking at the turned body, which is flooded with blood. There is hardly any limb and gut left, which isn't oozing and spluttering blood.

But this isn't what is making the driver of the taxi terrified. Though his lap is filled with splattered blood and his face suffered from shattered pieces of glass, what makes him terrified is the face, the very face of the man who has been the highlight of every news recently, the chairperson of Freedom Party, Mr. Anderson Herington.

×××

It is 8:30 and the crowd is replaced with police, forensic team, reporters, paramedic staff, and Mr. Hudson, the senior-most detective in the crime department who was dragged against his will by the sheriff, Mr. Douglas.

Mr. Hudson, a fine-looking adult with striking muscular features and protruding nose, is walking in the hallway of the penthouse as if taking a stroll in the park. Along with strolling, he is casually looking at the expensive decorative items and checking them up and down out of curiosity. There are ornamental vases, sculptures, and handmade artifacts which look expensive beyond imagination. All those things are depicting the interests of Mrs. Anderson, who has been an international icon for her exceptional artistic abilities.

Then he goes to the lounge and the attached bar which looks like the hub of Mr. Anderson for the whole night. There are empty bottles here and there and a single glass on the shelf. He goes inside the bar and saw pieces of glasses cracked on the floor. Carefully looking for the pieces, he makes his way to the collection of bottles at the back of the bar.

'Ravenswood Old hill ranch 1893.' He looks at the name and a desperate desire spark in his eyes.

"Ah, these riches." He puts the bottle back in its place with utter helplessness. All the while, he is stopping and smelling the things, like an empty glass, bottles, ashtray, and cushions. Then he moves to the pantry where he sees a huge stock of his favorite packed doughnuts and that is his limit. He picks one and opens it before anyone can stop him.

"I have checked all the rooms, everything is clean," the sheriff tells Hudson while stepping downstairs.

"Bingo," Mr. Hudson cheers when the ball of wrapper directly hits the goal, the dustbin in the pantry. He smilingly goes to the dustbin and peeks inside and the smile from his face disappears just for a moment and it is back again as if he sees nothing suspicious.

Then following the sheriff, he makes his way to the bedrooms, and they are clean just as how sheriff said but there is one problem with Mr. Anderson's room.

The internal decor and set-up are way too clean for a person residing with suicidal thoughts, Mr. Hudson thinks and sights but he doesn't express his thoughts to the sheriff.

After that, they both go to the balcony from where Mr. Anderson apparently jumped. The Forensics team is already there to collect the samples of fingerprints, footprints, etc.

Mr. Hudson looks closely at the glass barrier working as a balcony fence. Upon thorough observation, he sees some scratches at the edge of the fence which look rather off. He immediately takes out a green plastic paper from the forensic kit and looks closely at the footprints at the edge.

"Huh! These murderers never fail to disappoint me," he says.

Then he moves to the exit along with the sheriff.

"Look, I don't need fame, okay. I need spice. You understand?" Mr. Hudson comments disgustingly, looking at the dead body while casually munching on his doughnut.

"But this is the spice. Why don't you get it? Anderson Herington committed suicide? Seriously, do you believe this? Even I don't." Mr. Douglas stands right next to him, convincing him to take the case for investigation.

"Then that's your problem mate. I don't want to jump into a political mess. And that's the end of the story." He takes the last bite and moves to his 90's white Honda Accord.

"Hud-" Mr. Douglas almost shouts behind him and curses the day they became friends.

"I am not stopping." Mr. Hudson leisurely opens the door of his car.

"Ewww… A piece of advice maybe?" he almost begs, Mr. Hudson turns around and smiles in his signature sheepish way.

"Keep looking. That's murder. And…"

"And…?" Mr. Douglas asks with utmost curiosity.

"It is not spicy." He shrugs and drives away.

"You piece of …" Mr. Douglas stops midway just because of the severity of the crime scene and because he knows he isn't a piece of crap. If he said something that holds the meaning, but how?

The sheriff is in his deep thoughts reassessing the body and the height of 22 floors from where Anderson fell.

"Sir, the forensic team is almost done at the crime scene, and they gave a signal to dispatch the body to the lab." Bill, a junior under the sheriff's command comes but gets no response.

"Sir, we talked to witnesses, and they all believe it's a suicide based on what they have seen." He continues talking to get the response, which he got…

"NO! It's not a suicide." The sheriff shouts in frustration.

"H-How are you so sure, sir?" Bill asks cautiously because working with him, he knows one thing for sure, the sheriff's mood is like the weather of Alaska.

"Because that bastard is never wrong." Mr. Douglas points toward the gone car. Bill chooses to remain silent than ask the details about The Bastard.

"What about his wife?" Sheriff asks,

"Mrs. Anderson is still on her way."

"Ask the forensics to send the preliminary report once they are done with the penthouse investigation. And send the body for postmortem. I'll deal with the reporters myself."

×××

"As the witnesses said, do you also think Mr. Anderson has committed suicide?" The reporters bash Mrs. Anderson with questions the moment her car stops at the crime scene.

"Please stop this, she is not in the condition to make a statement right now." Mr. Clark, personal secretary of Mrs. Anderson stops the reporter's crowd from getting to her and makes way for her to get inside the building.

Mrs. Anderson, a fine-looking woman who hardly looked in her late thirties, is hiding her face from the cameras which are terribly smudged from weeping by now.

"The sheriff called for questioning," Clark tells Angeline Anderson while they are going inside.

"Tomorrow." She hardly spoke between sniffs.

"Sure, mam."

"You might have to leave the apartment alone. They think it could be a murder," Clark tells her when they see the red strip outside their apartment and a few members of the police department inside.

"Why would someone murder him? He was already a sinking ship." Angeline almost cries with teary eyes.

"So, you think it might be a suicide?"

"What else? We both know the crisis and the criticism he had been facing on the behalf of the party for the past few months. His mental condition was terrible, Clark and I had witnessed all those states of him."

"But still, suicide wasn't his type to end the life."

"I want to believe this as well, but here we are. He left me alone when we were in the middle of making the most beautiful decision of our life."

"He agreed?"

"Yes. Yes, he agreed, Clark. We were finally going to have our baby, but…" She breaks into tears all over again and this time, she can't even try to hide her terrible state. She is an explicit picture of devastation at the moment.

"Why…" She continues crying while looking at the empty elevator hallway. Clark holds her slightly to keep her from falling.

"I will get down to the depth of the investigation myself. And if I promise, I will make life hell for them." He gently pats her head and takes her inside.

xxx

It is late evening, and the wind is getting chilly. The old white scrap of metal in the shape of a car stops outside the big mansion. A guard in uniform hurries to the gate and doesn't even bother to ask for the identity of the person because the person inside isn't only famous for his work, his vehicle is also famous for leaving its mark wherever it goes.

Mr. Hudson parks his car in the middle of the way and throws the keys in the guard's direction.

He heads straight inside the mansion where a butler is already standing to welcome him. He guides him straight to a lavish lounge which is decorated with ancient relics and antiques. In the center of the lounge, an old man in his late sixties is smoking a cigar.

"Welcome, Mr. Hudson." The old man named George Flynn gestures to Hudson to have a seat.

"Mr. President." Hudson slightly tilts his neck, and there is an evident mock in his eyes, which the old man observes very clearly but smiles it off.

"Thank you for making time on such short notice." Mr. George, the current president of the country remarks humbly.

"You are not welcome. Let's get to the point, you have exactly ten minutes to convince me," Hudson replies bitterly while looking at her watch.

"Anderson Herington didn't commit suicide. He can't, especially after last night's meeting."

"What was so special about last night's meeting?"

"He joined the Democratic Party, and he was going to be the next prime minister in the elections," Mr. George breaks the silence, and it is truly a breakthrough for the investigation.

"Was his party aware of this betrayal?"

"This isn't betrayal, and no. No one was aware. He was going to resign from his position as chairman today."

Hudson is silent. Another picture is circulating in his mind based on the currently received information.

"Everything was going in his favor finally, why would one commit suicide at such a crucial point of his success?" George asks confusedly.

"Okay, before you lecture me anymore, let me make some things clear to you." Mr. Hudson starts to explain,

"First, according to my analysis, Mr. Anderson didn't commit suicide. Second, it was neither an accident because of over-drinking. He was a habitual drinker. Third, he died because of a brain injury, yes. But not the brain injury from the fall."

"What do you mean not from the fall?" The combination of revelations leaves Mr. George in confusion.

"He was already brain dead by the time of fall. I am sure the forensic reports will declare that fact in a day or two."

"Now the question remains, if he was brain dead, how did his brain suffer from lethal collapse? For that, I have two responses. Over dosage or direct hit to the thalamus. But one thing is confirmed, in both cases, we have a murderer.' He took a break and then continued. 'So, we are almost at the edge of how a unit, now the mystery remains for a whodunit."

"How?" Mr. George looks at him dumbfounded.

"I mean, how did you come to this speculation?"

"Oh, please don't call it mere speculation. There was a ton of evidence lurking around the place which only an amateur could overlook."

"And that was?"

"That…"

"I won't tell you because I haven't crossed you off the suspect list yet."

"Hah. I committed a crime and now I am trying to hire the best detective in the city to solve the case. Is that what you want to say?"

"You can do anything," Hudson replies bluntly and there is a pain in his eyes.

"Until when are you going to hold a grudge against me son?" Mr. George looks at him apologetically.

Mr. Hudson coughs slightly and looks at his watch.

"You took three extra minutes, shame."

And then he leaves as quickly as he came.

×××

The next morning, the sheriff's office is pretty much looking like a motel room. Someone is eating, someone is sleeping, and someone is typing a report while yawning. The mega case has turned their innocent lives into busy bees. Mr. Douglas is talking to someone when suddenly, the doors to his office open and Hudson makes an appearance.

Without any formalities or greetings, he starts looking for all the current reports gathered so far.

"What's the matter?"

"You're going to interrogate Angeline Anderson today, right?"

"Yes, but what's your concern?"

"I want to be part of your interrogation."

Douglas looks at his face and finds nothing but seriousness.

"You? Interrogation? Can I ask what made you change your mind?"

"No."

"Hah." *This man really knows how to piss someone,* Mr. Douglas takes a deep breath.

"I want to know," he insists. After all, it is his case; it is his right to know, if only the man in front of him could understand that.

"I want the forensic report as soon as possible."

"And the list of all people who had access to the penthouse."

"And Mr. Anderson's party activities and conflicts in recent days."

"Ok. Put a hold here. We are looking for suspects, does that mean, it's really a murder?"

"Didn't I tell you that already?"

"And who might have done it?"

"Someone from his party."

"Someone who must be the next chairperson, Mr. Carter."

"Mr. Carter would be the last person to do that if he knew the prospects of upcoming events."

"What do you mean by that?"

"My guess is someone who was loyal to the party and actually invested a great deal into it."

"That's Mr. Anderson himself, everyone knows that."

"From where he got the funding after the crisis so far?"

"His one and only wife, Angeline."

"I knew..."

"That she was funding for the party?"

"No, not that."

"I knew there must be a reason you are a sheriff." He smiles wholeheartedly.

"Why does this sound like you are disgracing me."

"Not at all. We will indict Angeline Anderson tonight. Wait for my call."

"Wait, what? Indict? Not basic interrogation?"

"Shhh... Just between us."

"Blimey!"

"When was the last time you saw Mr. Anderson?" Hudson questions Angeline.

"This morning before leaving for the gallery."

"You leave around 10 in the morning then why at 7 on that day? The receptionist and CCTV approved of the fact."

"A foreign delegation was coming that day."

"Your secretary didn't inform you while questioning. According to him, you were early because you had to check the arrangements for the upcoming event."

"Yes, that was also the reason bu-"

"Why are you sweating? We are not saying you killed your husband."

"What are you saying? I didn't kill him."

"We didn't say you killed him either."

"Can you please explain the purpose of this syringe in your apartment?" Mr. Hudson throws a package in front of her.

"That doesn't belong to me. My husband was an addict, and everyone knows that. He must be using this thing."

"This is the forensic report, just for your knowledge." The report says saying he was sedated. Not some random drugs which he usually used.

"I didn't drug him."

"We didn't say you drugged him. Why are you fretting so much?"

"By the way, this is your bank statement. Your husband withdrew 1.2 million the night before he died, I hope you are aware of that." Hudson passes her another piece of paper.

"I... Yeah."

"And this is your husband's infertility report, which you received on the morning of 31st December." Another piece of paper. All showing the motives which she had to kill him and what not?

"I didn't kill him."

"We know you didn't kill him. You hired someone to do that. And this is your phone records. Soon the person will be in custody as well and then you wouldn't need to tell us that you didn't kill your husband."

Angeline started crying all of the sudden.

"It was just an accident. I really didn't want to kill him..."

"He shouted at me, and I was so frustrated at his infertility report which he hid from me and all his political doings, and I just..."

"You hit him with this metal dolphin." Mr. Hudson puts a metal dolphin whose metallic paint is slightly damaged, on the table in front of her. "And when he fell unconscious, you hired a person to clean your mess who unfortunately cleaned it a little too well to leave a suspicion. Pity!"

DO NOT GO YET; ONE LAST THING TO DO

If you enjoyed reading *All Was A Lie*, I'd be very grateful if you'd post a short review on Amazon, Goodreads, or the platform you usually use to share your experiences.

Your support does make a difference, and I read all the reviews personally so I can get your feedback.

Thanks again for your support!

ABOUT THE AUTHOR

Everett Cannon is a professional banker and international businessman turned author. Already entrenched in his career, Everett realized he has a knack for writing non-fiction with the intention of helping others. It wasn't until he began inking short stories for his wife that he decided to turn them into a book and that he was pretty good at it. A father and family man, Everett gave up his career to raise his daughter and has never looked back.

All Was A Lie is his first fiction book, published in 2022.

You can follow him on www.everettcannon.com